The Minotaur's Son

& other wild tales.

Kevin Ansbro was born of Irish parents and has lived in Malaysia and Germany.

He is married and currently lives in Norwich, England.

BY THE SAME AUTHOR

Kinnara

(Paperback and eBook)

The Angel in My Well

(eBook)

The Fish that Climbed a Tree

(Paperback and eBook)

The Minotaur's Son

& other wild tales.

KEVIN ANSBRO

2QT Limited (Publishing)

First Edition published 2019
2QT Limited (Publishing)
Settle, North Yorkshire BD24 9RH United Kingdom

The author has his own website: www.kevinansbro.co.uk

This is a work of fiction and any resemblance to any person living or dead is
purely coincidental. With the exception of famous historical figures, most
of the characters in this book are fictitious. Some of place names mentioned
are real but have no connection with the events in this book.

Cover Illustrations by Kevin Ansbro

Cover typeset Charlotte Mouncey

Printed in Great Britain by
Lightning Source UK

A CIP catalogue record for this book is available
from the British Library

ISBN 978-1-913071-31-8

To my wife, Julie,
without whom none of my ideas
would have become words.

"Those who don't believe in magic will never find it."

Roald Dahl

The Siren Call

Fifteen years old and adrift from our world, with only a conceited cat and a tatty-winged bat for company, Jacob Fletcher sat high upon the frosty roof of a fisherman's cottage looking over a moonlit swathe of Cornish coastline. The cottage itself stood cheek by jowl with others, part of a crooked queue that staggered down a cobblestoned hill to the harbour.

Jacob, naked except for a pair of swim shorts and a diving watch, pressed his shoulder blades against the cold chimney stack and dangled his legs either side of the roof's apex. His age had remained unchanged in five years and, from his perch, the teen was afforded a panoramic view of the cruel sea that had engulfed him on a family summer holiday to Cornwall. "Why would anyone want to go abroad when we have weather like this in England?" he remembered his father declaring as he set up a windbreak on the beach.

Spread before him was a scene straight out of one of Dylan Thomas's notebooks: a brooding Bible-black sky and a hushed town tucked up in bed as the dew fell without a whisper. Jacob thought of his own bedroom in

London and wished he was back there again, playing on his Xbox when he should have been revising for exams.

As a mood of apathy prevailed, the cat, a Siamese with an emphysemic purr, slunk onto Jacob's lap while the bat hung upside down from a television aerial. In the witching hours there was little else for the trio to do other than idly survey the moon-silvered ocean. The night, as ever, remained hushed, save for waves slapping the harbour wall and the cat's vibrato.

Closing his eyes, the boy recalled for the thousandth time his father's panicked face on the day the unpersuadable sea took his only son from his desperate reach. Jacob remembered too his own profound feeling of disbelief as the sun dissolved like an aspirin while he drowned beneath the sky.

Despite the best efforts of police divers, Jacob's body was never found and so he existed in this quandary, trapped in limbo between Heaven and Earth, unable to move on from the seaside locale where his life had ended. The boy still held feelings of resentment towards his parents who, having shared a lunchtime bottle of Chablis, had been slow to react as he screamed for their help. His resentment might have lessened had he known that his father – and two valiant lifeguards – had almost drowned in their desperate rescue attempt.

"Mmmmm, r-rrrrmmmm, that's nice," purred the cat, enjoying the soothing stroke of Jacob's fingertips through his fur.

"Why does *he* get all the attention?" squeaked the bat, folding his wings in a sulk.

"Only because my family had a pet cat when I was alive," replied Jacob, craning his neck to look up. "Funnily enough, I can't recall us ever having a pet bat."

It was in the cat's nature to gloat and a smug smile grew beneath his whiskers. "I mean, what's not to like?" he said, admiring his claws.

Just then, their quiescence was broken. The Siamese was suddenly up on his hindquarters, vigilant as a meerkat. "Wrr-row! Look!" he gasped, directing an ink-dipped paw towards the open sea.

Jacob squinted but saw only a vast expanse of lustrous water. "Look at *what* exactly?"

"There! *There!*" the cat yawped, jabbing his paw with more conviction.

"Yes! Yes! I can see it!" Jacob enthused, spotting a large tail fin, silvery as a coin, flipping in and out of the sea's glossy surface.

"I also see it perfectly," squeaked the bat, keen to dispel the myth that his genus was as blind as the idiom suggests.

Gliding nearer to shore, the unfeasibly large fish tail revealed itself to be attached to the body of a lithe-bodied female who swam with the grace of a dolphin.

Jacob was up on his feet, hardly believing his eyes. "Omigod! Omigod!"

"What?" chorused the cat and the bat.

"It's a mermaid!"

"What's a mermaid?" they asked in perfect unison, but Jacob was far too awestruck to answer.

After some eye-catching rolls and a series of back flips,

the mermaid came to rest in the calm shallows of the seashore. Without a moment's hesitation, she pointed a ghostly, squid-white finger toward Jacob's lofty position. Against a backdrop of chimneypots and weathercocks, the boy winged his arms to walk along the roof tiles, returning the sea creature's unblinking gaze as he did so.

"Mmmm, nnnrrrnng, she's come for you, Jacob," said the cat.

"Oh, yes, she's definitely come for you," agreed the bat.

And this assumption proved to be the case. The mermaid sang to Jacob in a celestial voice that cut through the frigid air at a pitch that even the bat found impressive.

The teenager's companions were intrigued as to what he would do next. Other than themselves, Jacob had never interacted with anyone living or dead since his demise. They saw that he was clearly transfixed. The lilt of the mermaid's subterranean voice resonated deep inside his skull; her eyes, even from such a distance, bored into his soul and demanded attention.

"O earthly prince, cometh to me on the wings of night," she beseeched, beckoning him with a harpist's grace.

Jacob was in her thrall and, having spent half a decade roosting on slate tiles with only nocturnal visitors for company, was grateful for some fresh interaction. He alighted from the hip of the roof by stepping into mid-air and drifted over lamp posts, heading for the promenade, while the bat flittered above his head and the cat scrambled down walls, endeavouring to catch up.

Jacob landed weightlessly on the beach. The sea nymph luxuriated in the shallows only yards away, seductive and breathtakingly beautiful.

"Hello," said the teenager, adopting a nonchalant air, not sure how one should approach a mythical enchantress.

She arched her back from the water, revealing a torso as phosphorescent as the moon, and held him in her gaze, studying every detail on his face. "By what name be thee known?" she asked, wagging her tail fin coquettishly.

"Um, Jacob, my name's Jacob," he replied, transfixed by her oceanic eyes and trying not to stare at her breasts, which were buoyed by the water and veiled by damp tresses of tawny hair. The cat arrived on the scene and looked longingly at her scaly tail, hoping for the chance to bite a piece off.

The siren's voice wrapped the air around them in its ethereal chime. "I am Pendra, a maiden of the deep," she intoned. "And within so long a time, mine heart hath yearned for human touch."

Jacob looked at his animal friends for moral support but they were as amazed as he was. "Er, but why me? Why have you come to me?" he stuttered. She reminded him of the pin-up posters that had once graced his bedroom wall and fuelled innumerable teenage fantasies.

"O gentle Jacob, damn'd thou art," said the nymph mournfully. "Thy gods can only pray for thy bless'd return because they cannot see thee."

For a moment, Jacob's heart sang. "Return?" he

blurted, misconstruing what she had said. "Could that even happen?" He imagined this mermaid having the power to reunite him with his family and envisaged being restored to his London home, eating his mother's delicious lasagne at the kitchen table.

"Sadly, 'tis impossible," she sighed, "for presently thou dost lie at the bottom of the sea, eaten away by fish, thine bones undiscover'd."

Jacob's lips moved but the words refused to come. The thought of his earthly body being reduced to bones hadn't occurred to him, though it seemed perfectly obvious now it was brought to his attention.

The siren continued, her voice rhapsodic. "But think not of this, my prince. Think instead of a life with me, a life where thou art once more flesh and blood." Scarcely had the words been uttered than she balanced on her muscular tail and rose from the water, sweeping her hair behind her neck and exposing her perfect breasts.

Jacob gulped and his eyes ballooned. The posters in his bedroom couldn't have held a candle to her magnificence, and he instantly recollected how good it felt to be sexually aroused by a woman's naked beauty. Meanwhile the bat had become disinterested in hovering above everyone's heads and had come to rest on the cat's back.

Unable to contain her lust, the mermaid ran a finger across her blue lips and traced the contours of her breasts, all the time holding Jacob's rapt gaze. "O that I were an opened clam and thou a dolphin's tongue—"

The teenager was beguiled by her sensuality;

unsurprisingly, a host of impure thoughts invaded his mind. Pendra yearned for this lost human with all of her being and the pink gills on her neck reddened with desire. She extended her pearly arms towards him, hoping he might voluntarily join her and live a new life under the sea.

"Wraaow, don't trust her," mewed the cat.

"No, don't trust her," squealed the bat.

Then, with some difficulty, the mermaid flipped and flapped out of the water and onto the beach, whereupon the cat gave her tail an inquisitive sniff.

"Giveth thyself to me, sweet Jacob," she urged. "When thou doth kiss these lips, and if it were wish'd, thou shalt happily become the grown man whom the sea hath cruelly stolen."

Her otherworldly beauty was clouding Jacob's judgement. Not only that, his manhood had grown inside his swim shorts. When he was alive, his main aim had been to lose his virginity as soon as possible and here, within touching distance, was a nubile seductress eager to let him enjoy her body.

To entice him further, she faced the horizon and rolled onto her stomach, offering him a glimpse of the secret pink folds beneath her rump. Furthermore, she fanned Jacob with her fin while casting sultry looks over her shoulder.

The bat flew above the maiden in a figure of eight and the cat, without being noticed, helped himself to a small piece from her tail. "Mmmm, tastes much like salmon," he said approvingly.

The mermaid's voice was saturated with loneliness. "Cometh with me, Jacob. Cometh now and rejoice in our union, for it shall be timeless."

Jacob, not wanting to relinquish the certainty of his wearisome existence, took a step back. "I – I just can't, Pendra. I mean, I'd like to … er … y'know, I really would, but I feel safe the way things are."

Tears welled in the maiden's eyes. She had already placed herself at great risk by leaving the sea for more than a few minutes and the gills in her neck gasped for oxygenated water. It was becoming clear that this perfect human wasn't prepared to be her lover for eternity and an unmanageable sadness was already crushing her heart. "So shall it be," she sighed, raising herself up to meet him, pressing her breasts against his chest, her lips tantalisingly close to his.

"Eeeek!" shrilled the bat.

"Rroww!" wailed the cat.

Pendra's faltering rasp was at his ear. "Perhaps then, my love, a sweet kiss shall be our parting gift?"

Holding her in his arms, Jacob kissed the siren while her briny tongue explored his eager mouth. Such was his zeal, he didn't notice the saltwater tears that dripped from her eyelashes or that his virginal penis was more rigid than it had ever been in life.

In grave danger of suffocation, the mermaid peeled away from him and emitted a sonar wail that woke drowned sailors from their oyster beds. Without hesitation, she flipped into the lonely sea and swam out to the horizon with only heartbreak for company.

"Wow! How about that, boys?" whooped Jacob, punching the air and turning to his friends with a grin wider than his face. Sadly, his euphoria was short-lived as he immediately clattered to the sand in a pile of bones.

*

As daylight broke, police detectives were called to the scene. The skeletal remains, with a diving watch still loosely attached to one raw-boned wrist, were provisionally identified as being those of Jacob Fletcher, the missing teenager who had drowned five years earlier.

Chuck Montana in the Twenty-Second Century

Juicy Booty discotheque, Brooklyn, 1977

Resplendent in a white suit and contrasting black shirt unbuttoned to the navel, Captain Chuck Montana of the United States Spaceforce was having the time of his life strutting his stuff on a dancefloor that was lit up like a Vegas slot machine.

Soaking up the adoration of those privileged to witness him hip-thrusting his way through the Bee Gees' 'Stayin' Alive', Montana removed his jacket and waved it above his head like a lasso. "Dang, I feel good!" he whooped, bumping hip to hip with two ladies dressed in tight catsuits. "Whoo! Are you chicks diggin' this?" he shouted, before dropping down into a Cossack dance to a cordon of rapturous applause.

As he was taking his boogie to the next level, a column of blue light swamped the space captain and left everyone else in a state of suspension, as if a pause button had been pressed. A hologram of a communications screen appeared in front of him; on it was the disgruntled face of his supreme commander, Fleet Admiral Apollo Nelson.

"Heck, Admiral, I was bustin' some cool moves and gettin' my groove on, sir," Chuck whined, running a hand through his bouffant hair.

"May I remind you, Captain, that you are supposed to be the master of your own craft yet when I arrived on board just now you were nowhere to be seen."

"Just travellin' back in time and feelin' the funk, sir."

The admiral's face moved closer. "Are you chewing gum, Montana?"

"No, sir. No, I am not," Chuck replied after a discreet swallow. "I would not chew gum while addressin' my supreme commander, no sir."

"Hmmm," huffed the admiral, wishing as usual that his most highly decorated space trooper would spend as much time on his career as he did on his tan. "Montana, we need you to head up an important intergalactic mission. So, without further ado, I'm going to beam you up to the century in which you are gainfully employed."

Before his subordinate could reply, the commander had locked onto Chuck's pheremonic coordinates and conveyed him two hundred years into the future, directly onto the observation deck of the Galaxyship *Orion*.

Even before he had fully materialised, Montana was making his presence felt. "Yee-hah! Hold onto your panties, ladies, because Captain Chuck Montana is in the house!"

Lieutenant Unuru swivelled in her chair, fluttered her lashes and stretched her gazelle legs, hoping to catch his eye. "Welcome back, Chuck. The craft has been somewhat dull without you."

"Dang, Unuru! You are one fine-looking bunny. I know that in the twenty-second century we ain't allowed to talk to women like this but, man, you are as hot as hell, baby girl."

Chuck circled the deck, high-fiving the crew as they stared fixedly at display screens and star charts. "Give me some skin, McNab. Heck, do you even know what all those buttons are for?"

"Och, I canna say I do," replied McNab in a *Brigadoon* version of a Scottish accent.

Meanwhile the admiral was impatiently drumming his fingers on the armrests of the command chair. "Montana! When you've finished parading around as if you're a demigod, we have serious matters to discuss."

"At once, Admiral," Chuck replied, giving Leopard Lady an impish wink as he saluted the commander and clicked his heels together.

The admiral could feel one of his Montana-induced migraines coming on. "Take a seat, Captain, and do try to sit still. I take it you've met Captain Kowalski of the Galaxyship *Centaurus*?"

"Yes, sir. Yes, I have," replied his subordinate, extending a hand. "It's a doggone pleasure to see you again, Kowalski."

Kowalski returned Montana's handshake. "Likewise, Chuck," he grinned.

The admiral shifted forward in his chair. "So, here's the situation, Chuck. Last week, Captain Kowalski sent out a small peacekeeping team on a mission to the Planet Lurg. All five were captured and are presently being held hostage by the Royal Lurgian army."

Montana's interest was suddenly aroused. "Hey, isn't that the planet ruled by that foxy princess chick? The one with the rockin' body? Man, she is freakin' hot, dude!"

"Ah, good. I'm pleased that you are already a fan of Princess Galadua, Captain," continued the admiral, "because it seems that she is also an admirer of yours. Her specific terms are that we deliver you in exchange for the entire peacekeeping team."

Chuck was bursting with excitement. "Far out! Let me pack an overnight bag and I'm good to go, Admiral, sir."

"Not so fast, Montana. While I admire your almost childlike enthusiasm, I am very much a glass-half-empty person. The Lurgians are not to be trusted and I'm not sending you into a possible trap without backup."

Chuck hung one leg over the armrest of his chair and leaned back, smoothing his eyebrows. "Admiral, please don't send me out with that snail dude again. I gave him a hug last time and, man, I was covered in the worst kind of goo!"

"You're not getting the snail man."

"What about that dude with the big eye in the centre of his head?"

"No, not him."

Montana crossed his fingers and scrunched his eyes. "Please let it be pointy-ears and the lizard girl."

"How perceptive, Captain. You will indeed be accompanied by Science Officer Gurk and Elite

Combatant Zen."

"The dream team, sir!" cheered Chuck, while instantly forgetting their names for the hundredth time.

"You will also have a rookie in tow, Montana, so go easy. It's his first mission."

"The guy's a greenhorn, sir. Understood, loud and clear."

*

The Galaxyship's multiple-person conveyance chamber was not dissimilar to the make-believe one on *Star Trek* but, unlike the make-believe version, this one didn't do such an admirable job of teleporting human matter from one place to another, never mind from one galaxy to the next. The quantum physics were hit-and-miss, to say the least, and the rematerialisation process produced some adverse side-effects. For the first fifteen minutes transportees could expect an attack of severe hiccups and their bodies to be reduced to one-seventh of their usual size.

Chuck, having changed into a zip-up Spandex pantsuit, joined Gurk and Zen in the conveyance chamber. Zen had her game face on, whereas Gurk's was a mask of inscrutability. They were joined by Billy Bob Burton, a rookie fresh out of space academy.

"Honour above death, guys," said Chuck, trying to initiate a group hug that came to nothing. Gurk merely raised an eyebrow, Billy Bob trembled and Zen scowled.

The transporter produced a ringing noise, reminiscent

of a wet finger being run around the rim of a wine glass, and the team promptly landed on the surface of Lurg in a cloud of irradiated pixels. Due to them arriving no bigger in size than garden gnomes, they hid behind rocks for the first fifteen minutes, hoping that the sound of their hiccups wouldn't give them away.

"Dang! Hic! This planet is far out, man!" Chuck enthused. "Hic! I love hangin' with you guys! Hic!"

"Whether you, hic! Enjoy our company or not is, hic! Irrelevant," said Gurk.

"We have, hic! A job to do," Zen added.

"I'm too, hic! Young to die," Billy Bob wailed.

Unfortunately, they soon attracted a small contingent of chuckling crater pigs, for whom hiccups were a mating call. The sudden appearance of five alien porkers spooked Billy Bob into snatching his never-before-used phaser from its brand new holster, the result being that he blasted off both his legs at the knees.

"Arrrgghh! Arrrgghh! Gahhhh! Oh, Lord, I'm going to die!" he screamed, while the pigs scuttled to the nearest crater in fits of giggles.

"It's cured his hiccups," Gurk noted.

"Yours too," Zen added.

Chuck wasn't in the least bit impressed with the newcomer. "Uncool, dude! Now why the heck did you do a damn fool thing like that, rookie boy?"

As he spoke, they were all restored to full size, albeit with only six legs between them. The rookie was summarily beamed back to the craft, where he arrived screaming the place down and less of a man than he was when he had left.

Montana was determined to keep morale high among his remaining two officers. "Let's not let this setback ruin our day, men. Our mission remains the same."

"It hasn't ruined my day," said Gurk.

"Nor mine," agreed Zen.

*

"Behold, the princess's palace," Gurk announced later, checking his coordinates as a spectacular edifice loomed large in the barren distance. The three comrades strode purposefully towards it, keenly aware that the temperature on Lurg would freeze their eyeballs once the Piscean Sun had dropped below the horizon.

The palace was built on a grand scale and boasted a succession of domed rooftops and pointed spires. Its enormous gatehouse was guarded by two imperial guards, each of whom bore the body of a Nigerian bodybuilder combined with the head of a water buffalo.

"Halt! Stand still and declare yourselves!" the sentries bellowed in unison, crossing lightning spears that fizzed with high-voltage electricity.

"We come in peace, buffalo dudes. I am Captain Chuck Montana of the Galaxyship *Orion*, here by the invitation of your princess. And these are my partners, Pointy Ears and Lizard Girl."

One of the imperial guards spoke into an intercom and renewed his position. "Someone will be here shortly," he snarled.

The three waited patiently. As ice crystals began to form on their uniforms, the huge wooden gate slowly creaked open. Through it walked a humanoid toad and a vampire monk.

"Jeepers creepers! Someone sure got busy hittin' you two guys with the ugly stick!" whooped Chuck, clapping his hands together.

Due to the three pendulous tongues that hung from his slobbering lips, the humanoid toad was unable to converse as easily as he'd have liked. "Welfome, Thaptain Thuck Fontana. Sluuuurp! I am the prinffeff's efquerry and fee ith effpecting you."

Montana stood open mouthed and looked to his men for clarification. "What the *heck* did that toad dude just say?"

"He's the princess's equerry, and the princess is expecting you," the vampire monk explained.

"Then why the heck aren't you the one doing the talkin'?" Chuck asked.

"If only I knew," replied the vampire, rolling his eyes.

*

Montana and his crewmen followed their hosts through the gate and along a bridge suspended high above a moat. Flanking the grandiose entrance to the palace were two waterfalls that cascaded into the moat's dark waters.

"You did well to arrive before nightfall," the vampire said dryly. "The hideous flesh-eating mutants come out under the cover of dark.

"Heck, listen to you. That's like a skunk callin' a fox stinky," Chuck sniggered, drawing disapproving looks from his colleagues.

Once inside the opulence of the palace's main hall, Montana was in his element, feasting his eyes on a bevy of sultry maidens who reclined on an array of brocaded scatter cushions.

"This pad is freakin' awesome!" he declared. "These pretty ladies are wearin' next-to-nothing and I am totally cool with that!"

"Ahem!" coughed the humanoid toad, trying to restore decorum. "The prinffeth ith waiting for you in her beth chamber—"

Nonplussed, Chuck looked to the vampire for elucidation.

"He said that the princess is waiting for you in her bed chamber."

"Thaff what I thaid," the toad protested.

"It wasn't."

"I'll go on ahead. Let her know you're coming," the toad slavered, flouncing off with his pride wounded.

"Heck, I caught all of that," said Montana.

"He has his moments," sighed the vampire, turning his attention to Montana's associates. "You two are also our esteemed guests and, as such, are free to indulge in any of the palace's many pleasures."

Gurk raised an eyebrow. "A light meal and a glass of water will suffice."

"Same here," Zen concurred.

Chuck produced a hand mirror from his utility belt and checked his appearance. "You two wet blankets can do whatever the heck you want because I am havin' a good hair day and am about to have myself a hot date with a real-life princess. Lead the way, Fang Face!"

*

The princess's chambers were guarded by another brace of buffalo-headed sentinels who stood aside once the vampire monk approached. The princess, a woman whose beauty was revered throughout four galaxies, reclined upon a commodious bed. Apart from a horned crown, she wore a fur bikini visible through a floaty, diaphanous gown. Her voluptuous body took Montana's breath away.

"Hot dang! I am diggin' you, Princess Perfect!"

The princess's smouldering eyes lit up. "Captain Chuck Montana. I have heard that you choose your words wisely. One can only hope that you find a better use for that clever tongue of yours before the night is through."

"Yes, ma'am! My tongue is at your service, just as soon as you get rid of Nosferatu here."

Princess Galadua dismissed the vampire monk and poured her guest a glass of Lurgian wine. "Come, sit beside me, Captain Montana, so I may discover if what they say about you is true."

Chuck leapt onto the bed without spilling a drop and clinked his glass against hers. "And what do they say about me?"

"That you have phenomenal staying power and that you take women to the very heights of ecstasy—"

"Guilty as charged, Princess," he grinned, unbuckling his utility belt. "This ain't my first rodeo, ma'am."

"Oh, I'm well aware of that," she purred, unzipping his uniform and licking her lips.

*

After a night of unbridled passion, Montana was awakened from a deep slumber by the princess pleasuring him under the bed covers. Unseen, she worked slavishly to satisfy her new love.

"Hey, sugar lips, didn't you have enough of me last night?" he drawled, interlocking his fingers behind his head and enjoying the most incredible blowjob he had ever experienced. "Dang, Princess, I might yet decide to stay on this planet of yours, baby girl."

An attention-seeking cough caused Chuck to abruptly open his eyes. While he was being attended to, the vampire monk had stolen into the room. "Captain Montana, apologies for the interruption. I'm here to take your breakfast order."

"Hey, vampire dude, how's it hangin'?" Chuck winked, pointing to the rise and fall of the sheet. "I think that the princess has already started on her breakfast, if you catch my drift—"

A knowing smile inched across the vampire's face for no one had warned Chuck that the Lurgians were a nation of shapeshifters. The sheet lifted and from it appeared a face that caused Montana's blood to curdle.

"My darling, we could hath breakfafft together in bed," said the humanoid toad.

Doth Thou Thinkest Me a Fool?

Terry was already running late, and therefore grouchy, when he phoned his father. "Dad, I'm coming over right now to pick you up—"

"Pick me up for what?"

"Bloody hell, Dad, we've already discussed this. You're coming out with us for a meal to celebrate my sixtieth birthday."

"Oh, how lovely," enthused Raymond, pleased to hear his son's voice. "So it's your birthday, is it?"

"Yes."

"And how old are you now, Terry? I should know—"

"Sixty. The big six-o. God, Dad, how many more times?"

"Ah, that's right. Ooh, I haven't got you a card."

"No need. Look, get yourself ready because I'll be there in fifteen minutes."

Terry turned to his wife and two daughters, who were dressed to the nines and gathered by the front door. "Honestly, I swear he's getting worse. You three had best go on ahead and I'll catch up with you at Vivido's."

*

When Terry pulled up at his father's bungalow, his heart sank. The windows were still open, a sure sign that the old man wasn't set to leave. He slammed the car door and blustered into his father's kitchen, more irascible than before. The pensioner was sitting at the Formica table dressed in just a shirt and a pair of Y-fronts. "Dad, for crying out loud, you're not even ready!"

"Hello, Terry, it's good to see you, son. Ready for what?"

"My bloody birthday. Jesus, we're late enough as it is!"

"Ah, that's right, sixty today, birthday boy. Crikey, think how old I feel knowing that I've got a son who's sixty. I can remember when we bought you your first bicycle as easily as if it were yesterday—"

"Dad! Will you just stop talking and put on a pair of trousers?"

"OK, son, there's no need to shout at your old man. You know I won't let you down."

Terry put his head in his hands and massaged his temples. "I know you won't, Dad. Please get yourself ready while I close all the windows."

"Right you are," Father chirped, his blue-cheese legs tottering into the living room where he had draped his smartest pair of slacks over an armchair.

*

En-route to the restaurant, Raymond was first to break the awkward silence that existed between him and his son. "Could you stop the car near to the gift shop on the high street, Terry? I do need to get you that card."

"You really don't, Dad. I'm at an age where I couldn't give a toss whether I receive a card or not."

"Well, I care, son. I've always bought you a birthday card and I don't intend to stop now."

Terry regarded the clock on his dashboard. "Dad, we haven't got time for this crap."

A look of hurt clouded the old man's face and he placed a liver-spotted hand on his boy's knee. "Please, this is important to me, Terry. If you park outside, I'll be back before you know it. Go on, son. It'll make me happy to recognise your big day."

Terry pulled over a short distance from the gift shop, sighing emphatically as he did so. "Dad, how about if I dashed in to get the card? Save you the bother."

"Oh, no," Raymond sniffed. "You can't choose your own card. It wouldn't be proper."

Looking at his watch for the umpteenth time, Terry followed his father into the shop, where the old man scrutinised cellophane-wrapped cards as if the rules of time didn't apply to him. To Terry's acute exasperation, he even perused a birthday card intended for a six-year-old boy rather than a sixty-year-old man. "Our lovely little boy. Oh, how we adored you, your mum and me. She'd loved to have been here to celebrate your special day with you—"

"Dad, come on! This is getting beyond a joke. We're already more than forty minutes late!"

"Late for what?" his father asked, wounded by his son's tone.

"The restaurant."

"What restaurant?"

Terry arrested his voice before it could be raised and looked his father squarely in the eye. He spoke in a low tone, as if correcting a child. "Dad. I shall say this just once. We don't have time to look for a stupid birthday card. I have a table booked at Vivido's and everyone else has probably moved onto their main course by now."

At that moment Terry's phone rang. It was his wife, Beverley, who wanted to know what was keeping him.

"Is that *your* phone ringing?" his father asked, patting his own pockets.

"Well, it wouldn't be yours, would it?" his son snapped, as he answered the call. "…Yes, Bev … I'm trying … he's driving me mad … I'll do my best… Yep. See you soon. Bye."

"You didn't pass on my regards," his father grumbled.

"For Christ's sake, Dad! You'll be seeing her in ten minutes!" Terry's lower teeth were on show, a sure sign that his limited store of tolerance had finally run out. A hawk-faced woman at the checkout shot him a disapproving look and his father took a step back, shocked by his son's ferocity.

"Crikey, you're a bit grumpy considering it's your fiftieth birthday," muttered Raymond, shrinking into his clothes.

"It's my sixtieth, Dad, my *sixtieth*. Look, are you coming or not? This is your last chance because I am fast running out of patience."

"All right all right, keep your hair on," his father

croaked, offering the shop assistant a look of resigned embarrassment as he followed his son to the exit.

Terry watched for oncoming traffic and opened the passenger door for his father. Something had pricked the old man's pride, though, and he remained on the pavement, gathering his thoughts. "Why did you say that it wouldn't be *my* phone ringing in the shop? That was a catty remark, Terry."

"Because, knowing you, the phone we bought you ages ago is most likely still in its box."

"That's not true, son. I keep it with me at all times just in case you or Beverley were to call me. But you never do."

"Dad, I don't have time to stand here squabbling about the pettiest of things. Please get in the car, you're driving me crazy."

His father wasn't listening. He had spotted the red post-office sign and a splendid idea occurred to him. "Oh, look, the post office. They have a nice selection of cards in there!"

At the end of his tether, Terry slammed the passenger door with a vehemence that scattered a bevy of doves. "Right, that's it!" he snarled, jabbing a finger at his startled father. "I have tried my level best to get through to you that we need to get going but, oh no, you have to go and spoil everything!"

His father trembled like a fly caught in a web. "Son, there's no need to be like that. I'm only trying to do what's best by you—"

"Look, Dad, I'm through listening. I have a birthday

celebration to get to and I'm going on my own."

"On your own? B-but, how am I supposed to get home?"

"I really don't care, Dad. The bus stop is just there, that's if you can still remember how to get on a bus. I'll probably see you tomorrow."

Disconsolate and very near to tears, Raymond watched his son drive off.

*

Despite his misgivings, Terry's late arrival didn't hamper his enjoyment and the birthday meal proved to be a great success. His phone sprang to life just as he was spooning a last morsel of tiramisu into his mouth. "It's Dad," he said with a roll of his eyes. "Probably forgotten which bus he's supposed to catch... Hello, Dad—"

Instead of his father's, an unanticipated male voice answered. "Hello, is that Terry?"

"It is. Who's this?" Terry replied, signalling for the others to hush.

"Terry, my name's Gavin. I run the post office on the high street—"

"What's happened? Is my dad OK?"

"Unfortunately, your father was hit by a car as he crossed the road to get to the bus stop. The paramedics are with him. They did all they could... Um, there's no easy way to say this, but he died at the scene, Terry."

"God, no! No-oo!" Terry wailed. His family looked at him with consternation.

The sub-postmaster's voice began to crumble. "When I heard that terrible noise and saw what had happened, I rushed outside to help him. Despite his injuries, he still had the presence of mind to hand me his phone—"

"Please, no!" Terry sobbed, as his family crowded him, trying to understand what the call was about.

"I am so, so sorry, Terry. Your father must have been a truly wonderful man. As he lay dying, bless him, all he kept worrying about was the birthday card he'd just bought for someone."

Be Careful What You Wish For

"Aren't we lucky to have this second chance at life, Horace?"

"Oh, that we are, Ethel," Horace agreed.

Looking out to sea, Ethel and Horace, both octogenarians, sat on a bench on Brighton Promenade sharing a fish-and-chip lunch straight from the paper it was wrapped in.

"Neither of us could have imagined finding love again at our age," Ethel continued. "And here we are, one year later, sitting together like a couple of old lovebirds."

"And what's more, Ethel, I know that my Shirley and your George, may they rest in peace, would be happy for us too. Give us a kiss, my love."

With the sea breeze whispering in their ears, they shared a salt-and-vinegary kiss as seagulls wheeled overhead hoping to snatch a chip or two.

"I love you so much, Horace," said Ethel, gazing at his wrinkly face as if he were the most handsome man in the world.

"And I love you too, Ethel."

The silver-haired duo had recently married at

Brighton's town hall, a quiet affair with only close friends and family in attendance. Every day thereafter had been a blessing for the pensioners, a chance to enjoy their twilight years free from the scourge of loneliness. Ethel continued to work at a charity shop near the marina and Horace returned to his hobby of coin collecting, a pursuit he had been forced to abandon while caring for his previous wife as she had battled pancreatic cancer.

After they'd seen off the fish and chips, Ethel scrunched up the paper wrappers and deposited them in a nearby litter bin. "Shall we get these old bones moving and go for a walk on the beach?" she suggested, handing Horace a wet wipe.

"That's a very good idea," he puffed, heaving himself up from the bench on unsteady legs. "Oof! I'm as stiff as a toenail."

*

Their beach walk was something of a struggle, the shingle underfoot doing little to help their cause. Nevertheless, they approached the endeavour with an air of mild obstinacy and clung to each other for support. The sea had become as grey as the sky and they seemed to be the only ones on the beach.

Horace, though his eyesight was as poor as a mole's, spotted something floating on the shoreline. "What's that?" he asked, directing an arthritic finger towards the large object as it was washed onto the shingle.

Ethel prodded her spectacles against the bridge of

her nose and looked studiously in its direction. "I don't know, Horace. Is it one of those mannequins you see in shop windows?"

They drew closer and a saturated pinstripe suit came into view. Accompanying it, a human head, green and bloated, bobbed face upwards at the water's edge.

"Blooming heck!" shrilled Ethel, putting a gloved hand to her mouth.

"It's a man!" gasped Horace, stating the obvious. "And his head looks like a bar of soap that's been left in the water too long."

Though morbidly fascinated by their gruesome discovery, Ethel felt decidedly queasy. "I suppose he took his own life, poor fella."

"Either that or he got in with the wrong crowd," Horace hypothesised.

The dead man's right hand was clenched and Ethel noticed something peeping out from its grasp. "Fancy that. He's clung onto a pebble or something until the bitter end," she ventured.

Horace stooped to take a better look. "That's no pebble," he said excitedly, "it's the rim of an old coin."

With his shoes and socks getting soaked, Horace proceeded to poke his fingertips into the dead man's stiff grip, much to Ethel's consternation. "Horace! What the heck are you doing? You shouldn't be interfering with a dead body before we've called the police."

"But look, Ethel, it's an ancient coin – possibly Byzantine, I'd say."

"I don't care if it's a Fabergé egg, Horace. It's not yours

to touch!"

"But don't you see, my love? Something like this is what we coin collectors can only dream of finding. No wonder he didn't want to let go of it."

"Darling, I'm begging you to put the coin back in his hand before you get yourself in a whole lot of trouble."

"I can't do that, Ethel. It's of no use to this poor fellow now that he's dead, and who's going to know anyway?"

Much to his wife's dismay, Horace slotted the coin into a trouser pocket before phoning the police.

*

After the police had secured the scene and taken statements, Horace drove home with a repentant look on his face while Ethel fretted about what she called his 'moment of madness'.

"I don't know what came over me," he conceded. "I guess my excitement clouded my judgement."

They were told by a police forensic photographer, who didn't want to be quoted, that the man was a missing billionaire famous for becoming fabulously wealthy in a very short space of time.

"One minute he was working on a building site," confided the photographer, "and the next he was buying yachts and socialising with A-listers."

*

Despite his penitence, Horace was secretly delighted

with his acquisition. Later, while enjoying a mug of tea in his favourite armchair, he withdrew it from the trouser pocket for closer inspection. "Oh, it's definitely old," he marvelled, reaching for a magnifying glass and brushing biscuit crumbs from his cardigan.

"Older than you?" quipped Ethel, a smile returning to her face.

Horace rolled the coin between his fingers and scrunched his eyes, trying to identify its origin. "Arabic script, Ethel. This could be a real find."

Ethel limped nearer, her legs aching terribly from their walk. "It's about time I attacked your nostril hairs with the nasal trimmer again," she tutted. "You could paint a door with them, they're that long."

Horace fished a handkerchief from his sleeve cuff and proceeded to buff the coin, whereupon a vigorous plume of grey smoke billowed from its face.

"What the—?" Horace yelped, relinquishing the coin.

The smoke seemed to have a mind of its own, ballooning and modifying until it took on what loosely appeared to be a human form. Horace retreated into his chair, his eyes like saucers. He glanced at Ethel who was equally transfixed by the spectacle.

The cloud of smoke dissipated in a puff of sparkling dust and, from its midst, there appeared an apparition: a large man of Middle Eastern appearance, bearded, bare-chested and turbanned.

Horace had nowhere to hide and quivered in his chair, his tongue stuck to the roof of his mouth. The apparition folded its brawny arms and sought to reassure this new human that he meant him no harm. "Fear not, my lord," his voice boomed, "for I am your servant."

"M-my, servant?" Horace stammered, almost too afraid to look the spectre in the eye.

"You only have to ask," the apparition continued, "and it shall be done. Your wish is my command."

Horace looked to Ethel, thinking he had somehow remained awake while dreaming and returned his gaze to the entity that stood before him. "My wish is your command, you say? Like the genie in *Aladdin*, with his magic lamp?"

A broad smile broke upon the genie's face. He'd been hearing the same question time and time again for hundreds of years. "I am precisely like the genie you speak of, my lord, and I am also able to grant you three wishes."

Ethel had somehow come to terms with the fact that there was a supernatural being in their midst and she started to imagine an extravagance of life-changing possibilities. Horace, though, impulsively blurted out that he wished he knew the winning numbers for the next week's lottery win.

"Your wish is granted," declared the genie, producing a slip of paper that bore the six winning numbers.

"Oh, Horace, that was a bit rash," grumbled Ethel. "It's not like you to be so superficial."

The genie nodded in agreement. "I could build you a sultan's palace, or even an entire country, in the blink of an eye," he suggested, hoping that he might one day serve a human who possessed even a crumb of creativity.

"But I must warn you that I exist in this semblance for only one hundred heartbeats. Your remaining two wishes should be wisely, but expeditiously, chosen."

"Oh, dear Lord," Horace sputtered, realising that an unbelievable opportunity had landed in his lap and that time was running out fast.

"Think, Horace, think!" Ethel beseeched. "Imagine all the wonderful things we could do—"

"Seventy beats thus far," the genie warned.

"Ethel, I *will* think if you'd just stop talking," Horace muttered anxiously.

His wife, though, was far better at making decisions. "Horace. Wouldn't it be great if we could be sixty years younger and in the prime of our lives?"

"Yes! Ethel. Brilliant! That is a fantastic idea—"

"Eighty beats," the genie cautioned. "You have very little time."

"Sixty years younger," Horace blurted out in a blind panic. "I wish I were sixty years younger."

"Your wish is granted," confirmed the genie as Horace was returned to his twenty-six-year-old self, blessed with a slick of dark hair and an athletic body. His delight, though, was soured by the sudden realisation that he'd made a most terrible mistake. Ethel was still an old lady and he needed to act fast.

"Horace! You clot! Look what you've done!" she shouted with alarm in her voice.

Adrenaline coursed through Horace's young veins. "Please! I'm trying to fix this, Ethel. I just wish you'd stop talking."

"Your wish is granted," announced the genie before vanishing in an implosion of atoms.

Caché en Pleine Vue
(Hiding in Plain Sight)

The French hamlet of Culbiso nestles sleepily in the Rhône Valley, a medieval village brimming with cobblestoned streets and Gallic shrugs. A casual visitor might have imagined the three musketeers fighting against Richelieu's guards in such a place but in the year of our Lord, 2018, the most excitement one could expect to see was the community's annual fireworks display on Bastille Day.

As well as facetiously saying that crows packed a picnic basket before flying over Culbiso, outsiders also knew of the village's infamous dark secret; namely that its inhabitants lived in constant fear of kidnap or far worse. In short, Culbiso had a history of people going missing, never to be seen again. Local suspicion was drawn to the itinerant grape pickers who were billeted in the village for the harvest season but, despite senior detectives being despatched from Lyon to interview those agricultural workers who returned each year, no progress had been made. Unsurprisingly, alien abduction theorists had their say and descended on the village with film crews to interview the locals. More judicious eyes were drawn to Gustave Géroux, the brutish taxi driver once questioned about the strangulation of the butcher's wife in her bed while her husband was at work.

Local postman, Pierre Dupont – the person most likely to hear gossip but least likely to spread it – suspected Géroux was the man behind the disappearances but cautiously kept this notion to himself lest he suffered the same fate. He was particularly worried for the safety of Madame Pelletier, the old lady who shared her house with an intellectually-disabled grandson and nine cats. Unlike everyone else in Culbiso, Delphine Pettier had an open-door policy and Pierre saw this as a tempting invitation for the abductor to claim his next victim.

In common with the others huddled around the village square, Madame Pettier's wooden-shuttered house was every bit as stooped as she was. Her front door, flanked by recycled wine barrels prettified with pink geraniums, was left wide open from dawn until dusk.

Pierre cycled up to her house for his regular early morning *café crème*, determined to remind her once again of the danger in their midst. He propped his bicycle against a crumbling stucco wall and ambled in, announcing his arrival.

"Pierre!" she cheered, greeting him with a papery kiss to both cheeks. "Make yourself comfortable, my young friend, while I fix you a coffee."

Pierre removed his cap before draping his mail bag over the wing of an armchair and sinking into it. As ever, the house was dark; he likened it to being inside the belly of a whale. Delphine's thirty-six-year-old grandson, Milo, lumbered in, a gentle giant with the brain of a child. He offered the postman a sheepish wave and clumped back to his room.

The final rattle of a teaspoon against china heralded the reappearance of Madame Pettier, who wobbled in holding Pierre's coffee on a small tray as if she were negotiating the aisle of a fast-moving train. He stood up to receive the tray and then sat down again, taking care not to spill its cargo. His hostess reached for a switch under a tasselled lampshade, thus illuminating a miscellany of sleeping cats.

"I can see that something is on your mind, Monsieur Dupont," she observed, smoothing the hem of her dress over bony knees. Her eyes, still beautiful, sparkled in the lamp's glow.

Pierre shifted forward in his chair. "Yes, there is something on my mind, Madame. Specifically that, despite the danger we face, your doors and windows are always left wide open."

The old lady beamed, as if she found the postman's unending state of panic highly amusing. "You forget, monsieur, that I once fought as capably as any man for the Resistance against the Nazis—"

"On the contrary, how could I forget? You are part of village folklore," he interjected. "But that was seventy years ago, madame. If my memory serves me, you were ninety-two on your last birthday—"

"Ninety-three."

"Quite, madame. So, wouldn't it be wise to lock

yourself in until this beast is finally captured and put away?" Pierre shrugged his shoulders and took another sip of coffee.

Delphine shot him a dismissive look as two cats settled in her lap. "Pah! I have seen far too much in my life to be worried about some worthless murderer. I've slapped the faces of German soldiers, danced with De Gaulle, and eaten more sushi than the Emperor of Japan!"

Pierre waited his turn while Madame Pettier waved wizened arms as if addressing a large crowd of people. "All I am saying," he continued, "is that these are dangerous times. The killer could even be someone of your acquaintance."

"Exactly! He could be *you,* for all I know!" she enthused with a raspy chuckle.

Pierre, sensing that he was fighting a losing battle, finished his coffee while Delphine reached for a plate of raw liver slices that sat in a puddle of their own blood. She fed some to the cats and then, to her guest's astonishment, slid the rest down her throat. "Madame Pettier!" he gasped. "I'm fairly certain that you shouldn't be eating uncooked liver."

"Utter nonsense," she huffed. "I've enjoyed raw meat all my life and have evidently outlived everyone in the village."

Pierre shook his head and the old lady allowed herself a secret smile because each time she saw his nose in profile it reminded her of a parrot's beak.

After setting the cup down and slinging his mail bag over one shoulder, the postman bade the old lady a good day amid a cluster of kisses. With one foot on the cobblestones, he tried once more to make her see reason. "If not for yourself, think of the safety of your grandson," he concluded.

"Ha! Milo is big enough and strong enough to protect us both," she declared with a confidence that seemed to Pierre to be entirely misguided. So he donned his cap and, with a final shake of his head, sat astride his bicycle to continue his round.

*

Gustave Géroux, who had parked his taxi next to the monument to Saint Joan of Arc in the village square, regarded Madame Pettier as she watered the geraniums outside her house and fantasised about wringing her scrawny neck. Had she not looked at him contemptuously each time he passed her door? And wasn't it she who was the first to accuse him of murdering the butcher's wife? Knowing that he was staring at her, Madame Pettier glared right back, her eyes withering and defiant.

Geroux ran a strong hand through his dark scrub of beard and wondered, not for the first time, if she would be so courageous if he were to slip into her house and dispatch her as he would a hen.

*

Delphine's day proved to be no more eventful than

any other. The old lady posted cheques to four of her favourite charities, completed a newspaper crossword with consummate ease and watched an old Catherine Deneuve movie on the television. Milo helped out as best he could, emptying the cat-litter trays, of which there were many, and polishing the brassware. By the time Madame Pettier had awoken from her afternoon nap, night was closing in and a squadron of winged insects had flittered in through the open doors and windows.

Only at nightfall would she consider locking up, so she fussed with her hair and faltered to the front doorway while singing *La Marseillaise* under her breath. Outside, a halo of phosphorescence radiated from each streetlight – and out from the whispering shadows stepped the silhouetted figure of Gustave Géroux, his dark eyes filled with hatred and bad intentions.

"I knew you would come tonight, Monsieur," Delphine said icily and without a shred of fear. Before another word could leave her lips, she was summarily lifted off her feet and left dangling from his sturdy grasp.

Géroux kicked the door shut behind him and marched her through the room, throttling her scraggy throat while her feet twitched several inches above the tiled floor. It further excited the killer to hear her son's heavy footsteps upstairs as his murderous thumbs pushed deeper into Madame Pettier's crêpey flesh. He would deal with him, too.

Geroux's exhilaration was tempered, though, by the fact that the look in her eyes remained contemptuous rather than terror-stricken. "You still dare to mock me, you old bitch?" he hissed, intensifying the pressure of his onslaught as the few cats that were present let out a cacophony of wails.

He caught his ghoulish reflection in an antique wall mirror but incredibly saw only himself staring back. He performed a double take; the old lady's fragile neck was undeniably prisoner to his strong hands but he alone appeared in the mirror's gaze.

The brute was thunderstruck. A mirror could not lie and yet there he was, seemingly grabbing at thin air. His victim continued to stare at him with an unperturbed defiance so Géroux intensified his attack, wanting to see the old lady's eyeballs bulge from their sockets. Instead, a knowing smile grew from her withered lips. Meanwhile, all nine of her cats had filed in and gathered in a semi-circle, each sitting bolt upright on furniture tops to witness what was about to happen.

Madame Pettier, with a superhuman strength entirely at odds with her delicate frame, forced her twiggy fingers inside Géroux's grip and snapped both of his thumbs as easily as if they were wishbones. As her assailant discharged a wild-eyed scream, the old lady wrapped her legs around his waist and sunk her fangs into his brawny neck, savaging him as would a hungry wolf. She drank his blood so forcefully that his overworked heart heaved like a fish out of water.

Milo, alerted by the noise, descended the stairs only for his grandmother to greet him with a snarl, a warning shot across his bows. He knew well enough not to disturb her when she was in the middle of a feeding frenzy.

Géroux collapsed to the floor with Madame Pettier still attached to him. His foul soul crept from his dead body, shadowing the walls as it slunk away. She rolled from him and lay on her back with a sated smile on her blood-soaked face.

Milo knew the routine and dutifully transferred the corpse onto a plastic sheet while the cats licked the floor tiles clean of blood. Using a gutting knife, he removed and bagged Géroux's internal organs then loaded them into one of several chest freezers installed in the cellar.

*

Hours later, with makeup expertly applied and a tight dress hugging her slender body, Delphine stepped into the Rhône night air, once again the beautiful young lady who, from time to time, would mysteriously appear in the village.

Fait Accompli

In the living room of their sumptuous suite at the Artemis Beverly Hills, Charles Remington poured the oil heiress Veronica Meyer her second coffee of the morning. Charles, who was almost three decades younger than his beloved, fancied himself master of all he surveyed and enjoyed the exclusivity of this world-class hotel.

Dressed in a monogrammed cotton bathrobe, and pausing to admire the view beyond a balcony window, he padded into their spacious bedroom, balancing a small coffee cup on its saucer. "How are you feeling now, Veronica?" he asked in his refined Bostonian accent. "It's glorious outside, my love."

"Uh, still not good," she replied, barely able to lift her head from a swaddle of pillows on their king-size bed. The eyes that usually sparkled like emeralds were scrunched against the sunlight streaming through the windows. Charles knew those eyes as well as he knew his own thoughts.

He set Veronica's coffee on the bedside dresser and kissed her botoxed forehead. "So, what is it exactly? Do you feel ill? Tired?"

"Just tired, I guess," she croaked.

Charles fashioned a nest of pillows and propped her up. "The caffeine might help," he suggested. "Drink it while it's still hot."

Troubled by the sunlight, Veronica sipped the coffee while visoring her face with her free hand. Her lover, gallant as ever, closed three sets of drapes and plunged the room into semi-darkness.

"Bless your heart, honey," she sighed, a Southern drawl sugaring her old-money accent. "You must think me a terrible bore."

"Not at all," he soothed, relieving her of the half-empty cup.

Veronica closed her eyes, glad that the harsh light was no longer exposing her early-morning imperfections. Their whirlwind romance was into its second month and last night was the first they had become intimate. As she'd expected, Charles had proved to be an attentive, selfless lover and she didn't want his interest to wane. "You sure wore me out, lover boy," she chuckled, unable to stop her eyelids from closing. "I haven't been with a man in ten long years."

"The two bottles of Champagne we shared might also have had something to do with you being so tired," he ventured, grinning to himself.

"Perhaps I should get up," Veronica faltered. "Try to shrug this off—"

"I won't hear of it," Charles went on precipitately. "What you need is a decent rest, my love."

Dressed in a silk negligée, and having only succeeded

in raising her shoulders from the pillows, Veronica flopped back down again. Her beau draped the top sheet and comforter about her waxy shoulders. "Here's what I'll do, darling. I'll go swim in the pool and catch some rays, then I'll check back in a couple of hours to see how you are. How does that grab?" He leaned across to kiss Veronica on one cheek but she was already lost in a cavernous sleep.

*

Hours were compressed into seconds. Were it not for a full bladder that beseeched her to visit the bathroom, Veronica would have stayed in bed much longer.

The bedroom seemed much darker now so she called out, expecting Charles to appear in an eruption of luminescence with that film-star smile adorning his face. No response was forthcoming. Woolly-headed and yawning, she slid from the bed and inched her way to the drapes, barely capable of putting one foot in front of the other.

After sliding open one of the curtains, Veronica was surprised to find the sky black, as if it were night, and the swimming pool a ghostly glow. "Charles?" she called out, more in hope than expectation, for the room remained silent as a grave. She hit a light switch and continued into the living room, humming a dissonant tune to ease the strain of her bewilderment. "Charles, why have you left me on my own?" she mumbled to no one but herself.

Veronica sat on a toilet in the marbled bathroom,

allowing nature to take its course, and struggled to figure out why morning had become night in the blink of an eye. She also found herself prey to an incredible thirst and fumbled for a glass tumbler, which she filled with cold water direct from the faucet. Struck by an anomaly, the heiress stared with incredulity at her perma-tanned fingers; a white band of skin now shone where her De Beers diamond ring had been for the last twenty years.

Her voice trembled a little, though she was wholly unaware that she had begun to talk to herself. The heiress fished a cell phone from her handbag and pressed Charles' number. The line was dead.

Astonished that the phone's digital display read 19:22, she scolded the screen as if it might divulge her lover's whereabouts. "Dammit, Charles, where in the heck *are* you?"

Despite her annoyance, she started to wonder if something terrible had happened to him. Just as her exasperation was clouding into concern, a bolt of elucidation struck her. An instinct told her to open the safe. To her abject horror, its entire contents – her Cartier diamond necklace, American Express Centurion card and Hermès wallet – were all gone. In their place was a note that read: *You dumb bitch. As if I could actually fall for a washed-up old hag such as you! Thanks for the money, though! Love, Charles.*

*

Two days later, Kurt Henderson, pleased to have

ditched the guise of Charles Remington, smiled all too smugly at the news broadcast on a TV screen in one of the bars in Los Angeles International Airport. *"Police are widening their search for the ruthless conman who drugged famous oil heiress, Veronica Meyer, and made off with property and money worth $450,000—"*

The report amused him greatly, not least because the photograph showed him with blond hair fashioned into a preppy style instead of the dark crew cut he now sported. Gone too were the double-breasted blazer and pressed chinos, replaced by a hooded sweat top and jeans. His suitcase, containing the money and jewellery, was already safely checked onto his flight bound for the Cayman Islands.

*

Kurt's self-satisfied smile was still evident when, with a spring in his step, he traversed the jet bridge that led to his aircraft. A baggage handler, most notable for his orange hi-vis vest, held out a hand as if to greet him. Without giving it any thought, Kurt returned his handshake. He thought the handler's smile genial and yet, for some reason, something seemed off.

"Miss Meyer says *hello*," the man smirked, causing Kurt to feel decidedly ill at ease. Though spooked, he acted as if he hadn't heard the comment and entered the cabin through a corridor of lipstick smiles.

*

By the time his plane had touched down at Owen Roberts International Airport in Grand Cayman, Kurt had pondered the baggage handler's remark a thousand times over. Pleased to be on foreign soil, he resolved to ignore it and relished the prospect of enjoying his ill-gotten gains.

Pulling his suitcase through the green channel, Kurt could barely contain his excitement. The area was unmanned, just a series of empty benches. Beyond its unadorned walls he could hear the clamour of families waiting for their loved ones.

He was almost through when a white-shirted officer with gold-banded epaulettes stepped forward out of nowhere. "Excuse me, sir," the man said jauntily, directing Kurt towards a bench. "May I check your suitcase, please?"

Kurt's heart sank; he knew he would need every bit of guile to explain away the expensive jewellery which was hidden in his luggage. But, as the man rummaged through his clothes while congenially asking him about the purpose of his visit, it became clear to Kurt that the valuables were nowhere to be seen. *So that's it!* he thought. *The baggage handler. That fucking baggage handler!*

The officer, trained to notice the change in a person's demeanour, abandoned his routine small talk to study the passenger. Kurt, although he wasn't aware of it, was already a person of interest. "Are you OK, sir? You seem real anxious all of a sudden—"

"Hey, I'm fine," Kurt breezed, doing his level best to

conceal his anger.

Then, to his complete surprise, a small package, one he'd never seen before, was tugged from the inside of one of his shoes. Sick to his stomach, Kurt remembered the baggage handler's cryptic message.

Miss Meyer says hello.

Beyond the officer, he spotted a sniffer dog and, recognising a well-orchestrated *fait accompli,* acknowledged the triumphant smile of its trainer.

Kardashian's Bottom

Joyous from their hunting trip, Tipo and Yami strode into the jungle clearing shouldering a haul numbering two monkeys and one tapir. The men belonged to the Mikopo tribe and, save from loincloths fashioned out of plant fibres, both were as naked as Nature intended. Tipo, the sharpshooter of the two, had felled both monkeys with curare-tipped darts while Yami's arrow had seen to the tapir.

A Cessna droned low above the tree canopy; shortly afterwards, a photograph, glossy and dappled with fingerprints, fluttered to the ground before them.

"What is it?" Tipo called out, his voice tremulous and uncertain.

"I'm not at all sure ... it appears to be an image of a goddess," Yami replied.

Little did he know but the *objet d'art* clasped in his hand was a photograph of Kim Kardashian, slathered from head to toe in nothing but baby oil.

Tipo stepped over a monkey carcass to take a look. "Oh, her skin is so shiny, like that of a piranha."

"And just look at the size of her bottom," added Yami.

"Indeed. Her arse is enormous," Tipo marvelled.

"Plus she doesn't feel the need to wear clothes," Yami remarked, thinking her to be far more sensible than the few outsiders he'd met thus far.

"And let's not forget her shiny skin," Tipo reiterated, giving the celluloid an inquisitive sniff.

"So what shall we do with this gift?" Yami pondered, absent-mindedly stroking his nostril stick for inspiration.

"Yes! I have it! We must summon her! She will be able to stop the blue-eyes from building their dams and cutting down our trees."

"Or perhaps her bottom is full of fish?" Tipo speculated. "Enough to feed the entire village!"

"I doubt it," said Yami. "A goddess such as this must possess an intellect far greater than any human. We could exchange some of our botanical knowledge for a little of her wisdom."

"Or maybe she might let us daub patterns on her buttocks?"

"Perhaps she might, Tipo, perhaps she might... But let us celebrate our good fortune. Tonight we shall build a fire and drink *caicuma*!"

"Yes! And perhaps eat monkey?"

"Of course we will eat monkey!"

*

Sure enough, that very evening the menfolk left their small-bottomed wives to chat among themselves in the village longhouse while they sat under the stars, around a blazing fire, drinking *caicuma* and inhaling hallucinatory snuff that sent them all into a merry trance.

Kim Kardashian came to them in a vision, dressed only in a handful of parrot feathers. She bedazzled the tribesmen with her perspicacity and teased them with her well-upholstered backside. In fact, such was the potency of her dance that the men's loincloths were soon hoisted as high as flags.

Everyone retired to their hammocks later that night safe in the knowledge that the supremely intelligent goddess with the shiny buttocks would soon arrive to be their saviour.

Continuum

They were delighted with their choice: a scientist, one of the best in his field, from whom they had extracted data for a period of seven months. So pleased were they with his incognisant service to their kind that they thought to reward the human by helping him to realise his greatest wish.

*

2019 London, England

Professor Dominic Madeley was reading a newspaper when day inexplicably turned into night in the blink of an eye. He checked his watch. It had been a little after 1pm when he had last looked and now, absurdly, it was almost eight in the evening. Not only that but all the lights in the room were switched on, something he was not disposed to tolerate given that he was a conservation biologist with an inclination to save energy.

Over the course of several months such occurrences had been frequent and remained unexplained. The first time this anomaly had happened was when the professor put a spoon of steaming hot soup into his mouth, only for it to be completely cold by the time he had swallowed it. Then there were days when important parcel deliveries weren't fulfilled, even though he was most definitely home alone at the times specified and should have heard the doorbell. On two occasions he had settled down to watch a movie and found the remote control in his hand several hours later, still pointing towards the TV. He was left with no recollection of what had happened in the intervening time period and, at each juncture, his skin was left with the oddest smell – a pungent, burnt-rubber odour.

Though a rational man, Dominic was unable to fathom out the cause of these extreme memory lapses. His doctor was similarly at a loss to explain such an alarming sequence of events and speculated that Dominic being sixty-nine, allied with the medications he was taking, might be a contributory factor. Furthering the mystery, an MRI scan revealed an absence of tumours and two nuclear-imaging tests ruled out any signs of brain disease.

As is true of all scientists, Dominic was a curious soul, someone used to finding answers through a logical approach. Frustratingly for him, the episodic gaps in his life remained an inexplicable puzzle. The most perplexing instance was the prosecution notice he received for a speeding violation on a motorway that he had never driven on. Naturally he contested the charge but was astonished to discover that the police photograph unquestionably showed his car passing the specified speed camera and had also caught the unmistakable outline of his Van Dyke beard. A rabble of thoughts galloped through his mind that day, none of which made any sense.

He set down his newspaper and unconsciously stroked his wedding ring as he gazed at a framed photograph that took pride of place on the mantelpiece. It depicted Astrid, sultry-eyed and optimistic, expressing her beautiful soul through the lens while cradling their baby boy, James. His wife had been twenty-eight years old when the photograph was taken and had favoured a Farrah Fawcett hairstyle back then. Tomorrow, April 3rd, would be the forty-first anniversary of her death. James, now distinctly middle-aged, had grown up never knowing his mother's love.

*

1978 Zurich, Switzerland. Forty-one years earlier

Having met as science students at the University of Oxford, Astrid and Dominic's love for each other culminated in their marriage and him taking up a research position in the Institute of Biology at the University of Zurich. This was a selfless decision on Dominic's part, one taken primarily so that Astrid could live nearer to her family home. They rented a roomy two-storey house in the Höngg district of the city, and the happy arrival of baby James completed their harmonious existence.

One morning Astrid, with something troubling her, brought her husband a cup of coffee as he worked on a dissertation in his study. "Dom, please listen to me. I know you're busy with work but I have asked you time and time again to repair that loose stair carpet. I don't want to appear melodramatic but I tripped on it just now and was almost sent flying."

Dominic remained preoccupied by his typing and accepted the coffee without turning his head. "I shall do it when I can, darling. As you can see, I'm a bit tied up at the moment—"

"Maybe so, but one of us will end up taking a heavy tumble and then you'll sorely regret not fixing it."

"Have faith, darling, I'll get to it sooner rather than later. And thanks for the coffee."

Astrid planted an affectionate kiss on her husband's cheek and stroked his long hair. "You're welcome, baby. Call me if you'd like another."

*

It was April 3rd, 1978, the first Monday of the month. Fresh-faced Dominic Madeley was due to fly home to Zurich, having attended a scientific conference in London.

After James had woken from an afternoon sleep, Astrid carried him across the landing singing 'I Hear a Little Bell', a favourite Swiss lullaby. Distracted, she failed to remember the rucked carpet at the top of the staircase and tripped headlong down the stairwell with the infant still clutched to her chest. Sacrificing herself to save her baby, Astrid didn't let go of him and consequently her neck broke with a loud crack. After cartwheeling down the staircase in a whirl of hair and limbs, her lifeless body ended up in a heap at the bottom.

Dominic arrived home late in the afternoon, anticipating the mouth-watering aroma of home-cooked food. Instead he found James crying at the top of his lungs and his wife cold-skinned in death. He was later told that the fracture was high up on Astrid's cervical spine, which was why the injury was fatal. From that day onwards, Dominic wore his guilt like a cloak and never remarried.

*

2019 London Heathrow Airport.

A fond memory flashed through Dominic's mind of James when he was small, joyfully paddling his chubby little legs inside the yellow plastic confines of a large toy car. And now look at him, he thought, his wonderful son sitting at the wheel of an Aston Martin driving his old man to the airport.

"That'll be thirty pounds, sir," James quipped as he eased into a parking space outside Terminal 2.

Dominic managed a weak smile before venting a sigh. Today heralded the opening of old wounds as he was due to be a guest speaker at the Zurich Institute where he had once worked. Regrettably, the event organisers were unaware that today was also the forty-first anniversary of Astrid's death.

"Enjoy it as best you can, Dad," said James, understanding the faraway look on his father's face. "And give me a call when you're through passport control on your return."

After kissing his son on the cheek and saying his goodbyes, Dominic collected his small pull-along from the boot and trundled towards the glass façade of the terminal building.

*

The 11.50 Swiss International Airlines flight took off on time and the professor settled in with a gin and tonic and a paperback copy of *Planet Foretold* by Henry Drummond, the young sci-fi author. His enjoyment of both book and drink was abruptly disturbed by an unannounced bout of extreme turbulence, which led to the cabin electrically sparking like a Van de Graaff generator. The overhead lockers rattled violently, as did Dominic's teeth; his fingers dug into the armrests and his entire body convulsed under an extreme G force. He shut his eyes and prepared to hurtle to his death but instead a freakish silence ensued: a pure, unadorned silence.

He opened his eyes and was met with a fleeting normalcy. Normal, in that the aeroplane and passengers appeared untroubled, as if nothing adverse had occurred. At the same time, some things were decidedly abnormal.

The cabin was now noticeably filled with cigarette smoke and everyone on board was dressed in fashions from the 1970s.

The professor wondered if he was having another one of his episodes and closed his eyes again, hoping to shake off this most realistic of hallucinations. When he reopened them, the bewildering scene remained exactly the same. Even the aircraft's interior design had become decidedly retro.

Dominic struggled to come to terms with what he was experiencing yet everyone else around him remained unperturbed. Without making it obvious, he scrutinised his seating companion. Startlingly, this was not the same man he had chatted to before take-off. Whereas the previous fellow was a wispy-haired accountant, this guy sported thick sideburns that ran hedge-like on both sides of his face. He also wore a purple shirt whose extravagant collar overlaid a loud check jacket.

To his utmost delight Dominic felt youthful again, as if he had suddenly become an improved version of himself. His trousers felt tight against his thighs and tresses of hair fell over his eyes when he leaned forward. His hands, he noticed, were once again smooth-skinned and strong. He took stock of what was happening around him and concluded that he wasn't hallucinating after all.

"Excuse me," Dominic asked, touching his neighbour's sleeve and wafting away his cigar smoke. "I'm about to ask you a completely ridiculous question, but what year is this?"

"Are you serious?" the man marvelled, breaking into

a smile. "It's 1978."

The scientist gasped and put a hand to his mouth. "1978? That cannot be."

"Why can't it be?" enquired the man, furrowing his brow.

Dominic trembled with excitement and began to talk at twice his usual speed. "Nineteen seventy-eight? What month? Are we still in April?"

The passenger looked at him askance and blew cigar smoke over one shoulder. "Indeed we are. April the third, to be precise."

This simple statement hit the professor like a thunderbolt and shook him to his core. He checked his watch. It read 11am, which was somehow an earlier time than when the aeroplane took off. His mind raced through its gears as he struggled to adjust to the absurdity of this time-travelling reality. As the first officer put out an announcement that they were preparing to land, Dominic came to the realisation that he was about to be in Zurich on the exact same day that his wife was due to die.

*

Having cleared customs, the professor raced to the taxi rank, dragging his suitcase by its strap. His driver, Switzerland's answer to John Travolta, wore a white linen suit paired with a black silk shirt. Dominic beseeched him to proceed with haste, bribing him with the promise of a generous tip. The cabbie duly obliged and drove like a charioteer as a medley of songs from *Saturday Night Fever* boomed out from a cassette player.

The house was exactly as the professor remembered it. His mustard-yellow Fiat, once his pride and joy, was parked in the drive together with Astrid's Volkswagen Beetle.

The professor had hoped to settle the taxi fare as swiftly as possible but only carried Euros and modern-day British currency in his wallet. He looked the driver squarely in the eye, prepared to do anything to get out of the vehicle. "Would you accept my watch as settlement? It's worth substantially more than the fare—"

The driver turned the watch in his hand and scrutinised it as if he were an expert jeweller.

"It's a Breitling," said Dominic, impatience rising in his voice.

"Don't worry, this one is on me," the cabbie smiled, returning the timepiece. "If you're so desperate to get home that you are prepared to sacrifice an expensive watch, then I shan't keep you a moment longer. Good luck, my friend."

"Oh, gosh … thank you," replied Dominic, shaking the man's hand. "Thank you so much."

He had to be reminded to take his suitcase and strode purposefully towards the door of his former house, his long hair catching in a slight breeze. Pure adrenaline coursed through his veins and his heart struck up a percussive beat. With knuckles poised to knock at the door, he took a deep breath and dared to dream.

After a rattle of unseen keys, the door opened and

there stood his beautiful Astrid, her eyes as infinite as the universe, gifting him a radiant smile. "Dom! What a lovely surprise. You caught an earlier flight."

Dominic stepped forward, held her securely in his arms and released four decades of pain. His wife wriggled against his embrace, concerned as to why her usually stoic husband was sobbing so profusely. "Darling, what has happened? I've never seen you like this—"

"I'm fine, my love," he sobbed. "God, I've missed you *so* much."

Astrid wiped away her husband's tears with the cuff of her cardigan sleeve. She found the goofy smile on his wet face as endearing as it was confusing. "Come into the kitchen and you can tell me all about it, darling. But please be quiet as James is fast asleep upstairs."

Enthralled, and unable to tear his eyes and lips away from his long-lost love, the young professor nevertheless pulled himself together and sought to immediately undo the wrong that had torn his family apart. "Astrid, you know you keep urging me to repair that stair carpet? Well, I'm going to strike while the iron's hot."

Astrid eyed him with deep suspicion. "You're going to fix the stair carpet, *now*, directly after walking through the front door?"

"Correct."

"Right now?"

"Yes."

"Are you OK, baby? You really are acting rather strange."

"I'm fine, darling. Couldn't be finer."

"Well, I'll fix you a coffee. But please don't make too much noise. It took me quite a while to get James off to sleep."

"I'll be as quiet as a church mouse."

"I doubt that."

Dominic found his toolbox in the garage and from it selected a claw hammer and a utility knife. He also took with him a jar of carpet tacks. The trip hazard was rectified in less time than it would have taken him to write an email, and he cursed his former self for putting it off for so long.

"I am *so* pleased you've finally done that, Dom," Astrid approved, surveying his handiwork while cradling baby James. "It was only a matter of time before one of us would have taken a tumble."

*

2020 London, England.

The professor's doctor removed his stethoscope and asked Dominic to button up his shirt. "Another clean bill of health. Without wanting to put myself out of a job, it seems barely worth your while coming in for a yearly check-up."

Dominic slipped on his jacket and threw the physician a smile. "Considering I'm fast approaching seventy, I feel as fit as a fiddle."

"Then you are truly one of the lucky ones, Dominic," the doctor enthused, shaking his hand. "Oh, and please give lovely Astrid my very best wishes."

"I shall."

El Hijo del Minotauro
(The Minotaur's Son)

It was with much fanfare, banging of drums and blowing of whistles that the Circus Extraordinario descended on the remote Colombian village of Agua Mala one cloudless afternoon. Because Agua Mala was a three-day dirt-road drive from civilisation, its population of just 178 people were naturally astonished that their modest outpost would be graced by such a thrilling event.

The village comprised forty-three adobe houses, a rustic church, a makeshift school and a bar that doubled as a whorehouse. Its inhabitants kept pigs, goats and chickens and farmed a field of coca solely to keep the drug traffickers from razing their homes to the ground while they slept.

The locals weren't to know that Esteban Ortiz, a crooked businessman and founder of the circus, was drawn primarily to their blot on the landscape by fanciful folktales of Isidora, the winged nymph who was said to bathe in the river's malodorous water. A photograph showing her to be the size of a young child had recently been handed to the entrepreneur, providing him with unequivocal evidence of her existence. He knew only too well that such a remarkable specimen would make a very welcome addition to his troupe, should he be able to capture and groom her.

From a fleet of trucks and caravans there appeared a succession of circus performers, most noticeably a bearded lady and a three-legged Cossack. After spreading canvas sheets across a jungle clearing and erecting a metal frame, the ensemble worked as one to winch their grimy circus tent to its full height. And then, as trees reverberated to the sound of mallets driving stakes into the ground, the star of the show, the legendary Minotaur, made his much-anticipated appearance. After a swish of his tail and much flexing of muscles, he acknowledged the cheers of the locals who had cancelled a day's farming to catch a glimpse of his fabled animalism.

"*Ay, caramba*! He appears to have two tails," giggled Carmen Moreno.

"Puts our men to shame," purred Flora Garcés.

*

That evening, while the womenfolk and children watched the jugglers, clowns and acrobats perform, the men congregated around an improvised boxing ring to watch the Minotaur demonstrate his famous prize-fighting skills. So as to make the contests fair, the beast took on three *hombres* at a time and even boxed with one hoof tied behind his back. Even so, the fighting men of Agua Mala, emboldened by the consumption of jungle hooch and keen to prove themselves, were each soundly beaten and dragged unconscious from the ring by Father Pablo Vergara, who doubled as the village doctor.

Behind his oily smile, Esteban Ortiz congratulated himself on his business acumen as he disingenuously shook hands and slapped backs. He guessed that the yokels had very little money and even less sense, and therefore encouraged them to donate a truckload of coca leaves as an alternative means of payment.

Once the evening's entertainment was over the Minotaur, as naked as Nature intended and with his aubergine skin glistening in the moonlight, clumped into Pablo Zapata's bar seeking strong liquor and easy women. The menfolk, who had been licking their wounds and drinking themselves silly, welcomed him with open arms and without a shred of bitterness.

"*Hola*!" Zapata greeted. "You have left me without teeth, *amigo*, but still I am smiling. It was an honour to share the ring with *El Minotauro*!"

"Thank you," the beast replied. "And as a mark of my respect, I would like to buy a drink for every man who was brave enough to fight me."

Amid much back-slapping, a chorus of orders rang out. Even those without the courage to have fought a cat secured free drinks under false pretences. It was agreed by all that the Minotaur was the finest mythical creature the men had ever seen.

After girding his loins with several shots of rotgut rum,

the horned one was ready to satisfy his carnal desires. "My friends, it has been said that I can bed some of the finest whores in the land at this establishment."

Ghost Face, the albino, lowered his voice and adopted a sorrowful expression "But señor, the whores here are mostly unclean and ugly."

"Good. I like my whores unclean and ugly," the Minotaur enthused.

"Then you have come to the right place!" someone cheered.

With his pendulous penis swinging from side to side, the beast clip-clopped up a rickety flight of stairs led by Pablo Zapata's wife, who took him through a beaded curtain into a room where a bevy of sullen women reclined on tatty sofas. A collective gasp rang out among the group and many crossed themselves in silent prayer.

Despite his earlier declaration, the Minotaur chose Anna Reyes, the cleanest and prettiest of those convened, much to the relief of everyone else. Unperturbed, Anna led him by one hoof to a room that contained little more than a mattress and an oil lamp. Once alone, she caressed his horns and gazed into his tarry eyes as their shadows flickered on the crumbling walls. She felt safe in the Minotaur's strong arms and he promised her that he would be gentle.

There wasn't a condom in existence that could have sheathed his bovine phallus so Anna chanced a night of unprotected sex, little knowing that such a rash decision would change her life forever.

After two days, because he was unable to find and

capture the winged nymph, Esteban Ortiz moved his circus out of Agua Mala. The Minotaur was never seen again in the village.

*

Nine months later, as a heavy rainstorm battered the tin roof of her hovel, Anna Reyes gave birth to a baby boy. Father Vergara, watched by a crush of curious villagers, had to tether a rope to the boy's thick ankles in order to tug him from his snug captivity. It was instantly apparent to all that the infant had inherited more than just his father's proportions.

"I said he'd have horns," remarked Rafael Herrera, puffing out his cheeks like Louis Armstrong.

"Could they be sawn off?" asked Ghost Face, trying to be helpful.

"I'm afraid not," intoned Father Vergara. "The boy will have to live his life under a large hat."

"And, as he grows, the horns will only get longer," Pablo Zapata predicted.

"At least the child doesn't have hooves," giggled Salvador Seboso.

"Go to hell, all of you!" Anna shouted, comforting the chunky baby in her arms. "My son will never know shame for as long as I have air in my lungs."

At that moment, Sófia López, the village soothsayer, directed a trembling finger to a plaster effigy of the Virgin Mary. "Santa Maria! Look to the mother of God for she is crying over the birth of this devil child!"

"Relax," soothed Father Vergara. "There is simply a leak in the roof."

*

Despite his aberration, the boy was allowed to live a normal life, albeit with rubber corks pushed onto the tips of his horns for fear of him accidentally taking someone's eye out. His birth name was Toro Reyes and he grew into a fine teenager, courteous and strong, much-loved by all. The horned boy even became the first villager ever to befriend Isadora, the winged nymph. She had become fascinated by his mythological form and surreptitiously observed him for several years before breaking cover by circling his head one afternoon as he swam in the river.

"Wow! You're the fabled nymph I have heard so much about," he gushed in wonderment.

The beat of her diaphanous wings whined louder than those of a hundred mosquitoes and her iridescent toes skimmed the water around him. "If you promise to be kind and loyal to me, handsome, I shall consider you my friend," she said airily.

The boy was taken aback by her boldness. "You seemed to have already made the assumption that I *want* to be your friend," he grinned.

She drew closer, her glittering eyes staring into his soul and her voice harmonic. "It would be foolish not to, for I could be your best friend or your worst enemy."

"In that case, I would consider it an honour," he

replied. "My name is Toro."

She put her lips to his ear, her breath conjuring a small, sparkling cloud. "And I am Isadora. Be true to me, Toro."

*

Fifteen years after its initial visit, and with its customary ostentation, the Circus Extraordinario returned to Agua Mala. This time, Esteban Ortiz was intent on capturing not only the winged nymph but also the horned teenager he had heard so much about. His star turn, the Minotaur, had been shot dead during a bar-room brawl in San Andrés ten years earlier, and he needed some new assets.

In the presence of the entire village, Ortiz stood on the bonnet of a truck and puffed out his chest as if he were the president of Colombia. "*Viva*, Agua Mala!" he shouted and the throng, in return, roared their appreciation for the great swindler. At that moment, a monkey leapt from a tree and snatched his Panama hat then scampered off into the jungle wearing it.

Not yet aware that his father was dead, Toro hid underneath a circus caravan hoping to catch sight of him. His mother had already warned him not to approach Esteban Ortiz directly. "That vile man is treated like a god while we are living like goats," she'd grumbled.

As he lay unnoticed in the dirt, Toro overheard Ortiz plotting the kidnap of himself and Isadora with his henchmen. In the same conversation, he also learned of his father's death. With tears streaming down his face, he ran to the river to alert the winged nymph of Ortiz's despicable plan.

Isadora was unconcerned by the news but nevertheless pleased that he had rushed to warn her. "Fear not, Toro," she soothed, straightening his neckerchief. "An entire army of humans could not capture me for I have powers far beyond their comprehension."

"But Isadora, I heard them talk of large nets and tranquiliser darts—"

The winged nymph threw back her head and laughed. "I am timeless, Toro, and have lived through several centuries. These wretches are not the first to try their luck, nor will they be the last."

"I see," Toro marvelled, untangling a vine from his horns. "Would you be able to keep me safe too?"

"Of course. I promised you that I would be your best friend. No harm will come to you while you have my trust. And, in appreciation of the loyalty you have shown me today, I will grant you one wish."

"A wish?"

"Anything you desire. Something beyond your wildest dreams."

"But there is nothing to wish for, Isadora. I have the most wonderful mother in the world and you as my best friend."

The nymph was pleasantly surprised. "You are truly devoid of greed, Toro. Such a blessed rarity. But then again only half of you is human. If you yearn for nothing, then perhaps think of something that your mother would like."

Toro stroked his chin and pondered. "Well, she constantly wishes that we lived in a better house—"

"A fair request, my friend. Consider it done. I'll even throw in an additional surprise. When you return to your abode, you will see the power of my magic. It has given me great pleasure to repay your kindness."

Having said his goodbyes, Toro darted through the jungle brimming with curiosity and excitement. Upon reaching his home, he could not believe his eyes. The mud-wall hovel was gone and in its place was a modern house constructed from bricks and mortar. In addition, the residence had gained an upper storey and, instead of comprising sheets of corrugated metal, the roof was now a pitched affair with terracotta tiles. The windows, previously just crude holes in the walls, were glazed and curtained.

His mother rushed out to greet him, sending a rooster into a state of panic. "Toro, my sweet son. All of my prayers have been answered! Come inside and look what God has given us. It is truly a miracle."

She led him indoors. In place of a dirt floor, there were beautiful tiles, prettified with Oriental rugs. The boy sat on upholstered furniture for the first time in his life and marvelled at the framed artwork adorning the walls.

"And just look at this!" Anna squealed, turning on a tap from which a stream of hot water emerged. Toro was still trying to come to terms with the enormity of it all when his mother scuttled off in a flap of high excitement promising him that 'he hadn't seen anything yet'. She returned cradling a Chihuahua in her arms. "You know how I have always wished for a house dog?" she bubbled. "Well this little fellow is also a talking dog."

"A talking dog?" replied Toro, more than a little baffled. "What is its name?"

"Mind your own business," the dog snapped.

His mother's face was wet from joyful tears. "Apart from the day you were born, this has been the best day of my life. And it is all because I pray each night to our God in Heaven."

It took Toro quite some time to convince his mother that it was divine intervention of a different kind that had instigated her sudden good fortune. Once the *peso* had dropped, her eyes were alive with excitement and she sought to further her new-found prosperity. "Toro, as a small favour to your mother, could you please go back to this goddess and ask for a little more of her charity? What use is this beautiful house if I am dressed in rags?"

Contrary to his own instincts but out of loyalty to his mother, the boy with horns returned to the river and called out to his winged friend. She appeared before him with a hummingbird perched on one shoulder. Toro thanked her for her generosity and steeled himself to capitalise on her kindness in a way that felt unseemly. He took the plunge and entreated Isadora to use her magic to provide his mother with a set of new clothes.

As he had feared, her expression was one of palpable disappointment. "Toro. I plainly said that I would grant you just one wish. Have I not been true to my word?"

"If it were up to me, I wouldn't ask," he squirmed.

"But my mother, she is very insistent."

"Very well," Isadora huffed. "Go home to your mother. I have just equipped her with a wardrobe of new clothes. But I warn you not to take my friendship for granted."

Toro bowed his head in deference. "I won't. Thank you, señorita. Thank you from the bottom of my heart."

Hoping she would induce envy in all who passed by, Toro's mother was posing in new clothes outside her house when he returned. Instead of walking barefoot, she was now standing in stiletto heels totally unsuited to the terrain, and slinking around in the kind of dress that the villagers had only seen in magazines.

"My son! My wonderful son!" she yelled, waving a Gucci handbag as if sending a semaphore message. "I have just one last request and then I will be the happiest lady in all of Colombia. Please ask this kind-hearted goddess if she could gift me enough money to allow me a comfortable life until I die. What use is this magnificent house and these fancy clothes if I still have to sell my body to put food on the table?"

Filled with foreboding, Toro turned on his heels, traipsed through the jungle and returned to the riverbank. High above, birds squabbled in the trees and Isadora greeted him with a frown. "I know what you are going to say before you even say it," she reproached.

The boy's discomfort was such that he couldn't look his winged friend in the eye. "This will be the last time I impose upon you. Please believe me," he entreated, "I do this not for myself but for the love of my mother."

"A mother who does not know when to count her

blessings," Isadora scolded.

"I'm certain that this will be the end of it," Toro sighed. "Please indulge me this one last time and I promise that I will be the best friend you could ever wish for."

"Fine. It is done," said Isadora, her mood brightening. "So, perhaps I can do something for you?"

"For me?" Toro gasped, delighted that her displeasure was so short-lived. "What did you have in mind?"

She circled him, her wings a diaphanous blur. "Would you like me to grant you the ability to fly? I'm sure it would mean more to you than anything materialistic."

"Fly? Oh, yes please!" exclaimed the boy. "That's if you don't mind, of course. What a thrill it must be to soar above the clouds!"

Isadora smiled warmly and cast a spell that gave him wings powerful enough to lift his sturdy frame off the ground. "Let us fly up to the top of that mountain," she enthused. "You'll find it as natural as walking."

The nymph's confidence in Toro's fledgling ability was not misplaced. After a few preliminary flaps, he propelled himself skyward with consummate ease. In no time at all he was level with the treetops. They flew together over the jungle canopy and gained altitude, heading towards the snow-capped mountain in the distance.

"How does it feel?" she giggled, deriving a great deal of satisfaction from seeing the huge smile on his face.

"This is by far the best experience of my life," he yelled above the beat of his wings as he grew in confidence and learned to glide on thermal columns.

Isadora signalled for him to alight on a mountain

ledge. Ice crystals formed on his horns as he stood on their lofty perch. "Look at you shivering," she chuckled. "We had better fly back down before you freeze to death."

He was first to leap from the precipice and hurtled downward at breakneck speed. "Whoo-hoo!" he whooped, the rush of air wobbling his cheeks and blurring his vision. Isadora flew alongside and they exchanged smiles. "I seem to be going rather too fast!" he shouted, unable to slow his rapid descent.

"Flap your arms as well as your wings," Isadora suggested. Her expression was serene whereas his was one of pure terror.

"It's not working!" he shrieked, flapping his arms for all he was worth. "Help me, Isadora! It's not working!"

"I did warn you that I could be your worst enemy," she purred, arrowing towards the ground with him.

Seconds from impact, and with his life flashing before him, Toro's descent was abruptly arrested, as if he'd been grabbed by a giant's hand. His heart was beating through his chest as he hovered above the very rocks that would have smashed his body into pieces.

Isadora's voice was thick with menace. "I hope that today you have learned not to take my friendship for granted. Go back to your mother, boy, and ponder the moral of this story."

When Toro returned home, it was to the whitewashed hovel he had been born in. His distraught mother was on her knees in the dirt, dressed in rags and cursing her unanticipated misfortune.

*

The circus performers, wondering why Esteban Ortiz was late opening the show, trooped to his trailer. He and his villainous associates were still in their seats, black-tongued and turned to stone.

The Show-off

Norwich, England

I might have had more success holding back the tide than trying to decline Penelope's invitation to her annual summer cocktail party.

"Oh, you must come, Kevin," she entreated over the phone. "You could give a talk about your latest book."

"I'd rather not," I replied.

Penelope was not to be denied. "Oh, don't be such a bloody sourpuss. It'll be a fabulous evening and everyone will be delighted to meet Kevin Ansbro, the famous author."

"Er, I'm not famous, Penny. In fact, I'm not even famous in Norwich! Remember that book signing? They were hardly queuing out the door."

"Nonsense. Now there are some really fascinating people coming, most of whom you'll love."

"You think?"

Penelope paused before playing her perennial trump card. "Stephen Fry might be coming."

"Oh, Penny, you invite him every year," I groaned.

"And, to my recollection, he's never turned up once. I bet you've not even had a reply."

"Omigod, you are such a Doubting Thomas, Kevin. Just turn up on the night, suited and booted, or I will come over to your house and fight you on the doorstep in front of Julie."

A broad smile spread across my face. "In that case, I accept your kind offer."

*

I first met Penelope in the '80s when I fleetingly worked as a young bartender, shaking cocktails at an American-themed restaurant in Norwich city centre. My mixology skills were non-existent so I learned as I went along – the owners were clearly desperate. I lasted less than a week before being justifiably fired for gross misconduct because I drank more cocktails than I served.

Penelope rocked up to the bar one day wearing black lipstick, fingerless lace gloves and a rag tied into a bow on top of her head; it was a look that seemed entirely out of kilter with her upmarket accent. She was a friend to men and an enthusiastic lover of women. We got on famously and had remained buddies ever since.

And she absolutely did have Stephen Fry's coveted phone number in her contacts list. Penelope was his makeup artist on a TV sketch show in the '90s and, so as not to abuse his benevolence, only texted him once a year in the slim hope that he might attend one of her soirées.

*

My wife had opportunely picked that weekend to fly over to Amsterdam with friends, so I stood alone in Penelope's Grade II listed Georgian townhouse, resplendent in a navy blue suit that I only trotted out for special occasions.

As usual, our hostess had gone to a great deal of effort. A banqueting table, laid with a crisp, white tablecloth, was bedecked with floral arrangements and a spectacular array of hors d'oeuvres. Queues of Champagne flutes were filled to varying levels with Prosecco, and the cutlery was swaddled in linen napkins. Pleasingly, an agreeable selection of guests populated the large drawing room and, as promised, an air of cordiality prevailed.

I was on my second glass of Rioja and could not have been happier when Penelope sidled up to me holding a bottle of fizz, its label conveniently obscured by a napkin. "I told you this would be fun," she chirped. "Could I interest you in a glass of Champagne?"

"You and I both know it's Prosecco, Penny," I winked. "But I'm fine with my glass of red."

"Ooh, hark at you! I knew you when you only drank Guinness, you absolute snob."

"And I knew you when the police almost arrested you for being steaming drunk and snogging a half-naked woman in the fountain outside C&A."

Penelope's feline eyes sparkled. "God, yeah. Bloody

police, spoiling my midnight lechery."

Casting the banter to one side, I adopted a solicitous tone and thanked my fabulous friend for inviting me. "And look at this amazing spread," I added. "You've truly pulled out all the stops, Penny, and I'm having a great time."

"You're welcome, sweetie. I'm pleased you came."

It was then that he held me in his gaze, a great overbearing ruddy-faced lummox of a man in desperate need of someone to talk to. Once locked onto my coordinates, there was no stopping him. For a big lump he was fast on his feet, moving loose limbed through the crowd like a gibbon swinging through trees.

Almost barging Penelope aside, he was upon me, shiny-suited and offering a meaty hand. "Name's Matt," he grunted, fixing me with an uncomfortably penetrating stare.

Matt the prat, I thought to myself.

"Pleased to meet you, Matt," I said, lying through my teeth. "I'm Kevin."

I cast an eye over him, using word association to consign his name to memory. Though middle-aged, his hair was as black as Superman's and an unremarkable moustache clung to his top lip like moss to a roof tile. He was oafish yet wore a well-tailored suit, putting me in mind of someone who had won the National Lottery. It didn't surprise me one bit to see an ostentatious watch, the size of a coaster, emerge from his cufflinked sleeves.

Penelope moved quietly behind him and formed her hand into a mime of a quacking beak, indicating to me that he was something of a windbag. "Good luck," she mouthed before leaving me at Matt's mercy. I was on high alert and my inner voice scrabbled up to the control deck.

"So, how did you get here tonight, Kevin?" he asked, his voice as clamorous as a church bell.

Huh? Such a bizarre opening question.

"By taxi," I answered plainly, wondering where this was leading. *Why? Did you rock up in a jewelled chariot pulled by unicorns?*

Matt drew himself to his full height and puffed out his chest. His shirt was so white I thought it might snowblind me. "I'm the owner of the Bentley that you no doubt noticed when you arrived," he brayed.

Oh, dear God, he's even worse than I envisaged.

"I didn't see any Bentley," I replied, furrowing my brow.

"Didn't see it? You couldn't bloody miss it!" he squealed. "I parked it right next to the front door. Aegean blue, top of the range, six-litre engine. Cost me over 170 grand."

What an idiot.

"Sorry, I'm just not into cars, Matt," I replied, hoping to burst his bubble. "A Batmobile might have grabbed my attention, though."

"The birds love it," he boasted.

Birds. Such a charmer.

I noticed with dismay that he was clenching his Champagne flute as if it were a beer bottle. I imagined he was the sort of person who would leave his knife and fork scattered across his dinner plate.

Glancing to my left, I spotted a bookish young man standing on his own with a hardback copy of *One Hundred Years of Solitude* tucked under one arm. How I wished I was having a conversation with that guy rather than this dipstick.

Expecting to impress me further with his braggadocio, Matt was out of the traps again. "I'm the CEO of my own call centre," he crowed.

I answered him with a thin smile and wondered if he had ever appreciated the lilt of birdsong on a summer's day.

A tide of glee flooded his piercing eyes. "Would you like to know how much I earned last year?"

"Not especially," I sighed. His white shirt was stretched tight over his kettle-drum belly and I somehow resisted the urge to tip red wine over it.

"Three hundred grand," he beamed.

"Bully for you," I retorted, showing him the bored face I reserve for narcissists and imbeciles.

You are going to get a glass of red over you if you don't shut up, you moron.

I considered his shoes which were as pointy as a curlew's beak. And they had a buckle on them! Who the hell has buckles on their shoes outside of a Brothers Grimm fairy tale?

Matt wore his ego like a crown. "As a matter of fact, I just picked up a prestigious award for being the top entrepreneur in Norfolk," he trumpeted.

Well, aren't you a clever boy?

The show-off pulled back his shirt cuff. "Do you like watches, Kevin?"

"Yes, I do. They're great for telling the time."

"This one was only eleven grand," he clucked. "I've left the expensive ones at home."

Jee-sus. How much longer are you going to put up with this, Kev?

"So what do you do?" Matt asked, astonishing me by showing an interest in someone other than himself.

"I'm an author."

His look was one of disgust, as if I'd just admitted to being a necrophiliac. "An author?" he snorted. "Shouldn't think there's much money in that, is there? You should come and work for me."

My hackles were well and truly raised. "It's hardly a business opportunity, Matt, it's a calling. Writing is my passion." His shirt looked beautifully crisp and white. My wine glass was still half full.

Go on, Kev, you know you want to.

"I value the kindness of strangers more than I do material possessions," I continued, taking the moral high ground.

Matt scrunched his face as if he had just sucked on a lemon. "Fuck me. Are you some kind of hippy?"

One more stupid word, mate, and I'm going to chuck Rioja all over your nice shirt.

"Hardly. I'm as much a hippy as you are a decent human being," I countered.

The self-obsessed prat ignored everything I'd just said. Of course he did; after all, the words hadn't come from his mouth. "So are you any good then?" he asked.

"No, I'm crap, Matt. I just like the humiliation it brings."

Undaunted, he set down his Champagne flute and shovelled salted peanuts into his overworked mouth. "Y'know, I often think that I should write an autobiography about my life. It would make a very interesting read—"

God Almighty! What a pillock.

"Yes, you really must do that," I grinned. "I should imagine the literary world cannot wait to hear all about your prized Bentley, your watch collection, and how much money you earned last year."

I noticed with relish that a line of black hair dye had begun to trickle down Matt's sweaty forehead and that the strings of his smile were suddenly cut.

"You're a sarcastic fucker," he huffed, jabbing a fat finger into my chest. "I'm not sure I like your tone."

"Aww, that's a pity, Matt, because there's plenty more where that came from."

Do it, Kev!

OK, I will!

"Oh, whoops-a-daisy. I've just spilled red wine all over your nice white shirt. How terribly clumsy of me."

Matt stepped back, wide-eyed, as if he had trodden in something nasty. "You bastard! You fucking did that on purpose!"

"On purpose? How could you even think such a thing? And I'll bet it's an expensive shirt too. You must send me the dry-cleaning bill."

Penelope had evidently witnessed what had just occurred and erupted in a fit of giggles whereupon he scorched her with his furious gaze. "I'm not staying here a moment longer!" he thundered, shoving guests out of his way and heading for the hallway. "You lot don't deserve me!"

"Oh, but I never got to see your Bentley!" I cried out after him. Sadly, the fella was in no mood to stop.

Rather than being angry, Penelope hung an arm over my shoulder and thanked me. "You've actually done me a huge favour, Kevin. I've been trying to get rid of that egomaniac for years."

"I'll see to it that your carpet is sorted out," I promised, pointing guiltily to the dark stain on her Axminster.

"God, I shouldn't worry," she replied, handing me a glass of Prosecco. "It's being steam-cleaned next week."

*

My evening thereafter was truly marvellous. You might be pleased to learn that I managed to have an enjoyable chat with the bookish young man about Gabriel García Márquez and all things literature. I even succeeded in remembering the names of everyone I had been introduced to, which was no small feat since my mind is like a sieve. And then, just when I thought the night couldn't get any better, in loped none other than Mr Stephen Fry!

A Matter of Honour

Allied Turkey, 1854
The British army hospital at Scutari, during the Crimean
War

With the digits of his left hand amputated, and to the background sound of terrible screams, Captain Hugo Pinkerton woke from a chloroform-induced sleep in the army's makeshift hospital. He was vaguely aware of a pretty nurse standing over him, her face no more than a distorted mirage as the effects of the drug wore off.

Once he had regained consciousness the vision spoke to him, her voice as soothing as a lullaby. "Welcome back, Captain Pinkerton," she smiled.

Despite running a fever, the young officer was instantly beguiled. "Did my heart love till now? Forswear it sight. For I never saw beauty till this night."

"Bravo, fair Romeo, but you must conserve your energy," the nurse chuckled. "You should be pleased to know that the surgeon has only cut away what was absolutely necessary."

The officer raised his left arm; on its extremity was a stump wrapped in a blood-soaked bandage. "Good gracious!" he exclaimed. "My fingers lopped off like branches from a tree."

The nurse held his good hand. "I dare say your life will continue much as normal," she breezed.

"Well, I shan't be able to play the violin again but you are right, of course. And in any case, I care less about losing my fingers than I did about losing my beautiful horse. There was no time to thank him for his service as he died beneath me, and I freely admit to shedding a tear for him once the battle had ended."

The captain was a cavalryman with the 11th Hussars and had recently been part of the suicidal charge on Russian lines during the Battle of Balaclava, where he had galloped into a forest of lances under a hail of bullets and cannonballs. Though his steed was shot down, Pinkerton had briskly mounted a riderless horse and resumed fighting.

As if to remind the officer of his good fortune, a wounded soldier was laid on the bed next to him, his uniform shredded with bullet holes and hair crawling with lice. All around men were dying, as much from cholera and typhoid as they were from their terrible injuries, while the medical team did their best in unsanitary conditions.

"Upon my soul!" Pinkerton exclaimed, seeing a rat scuttle across his blanket. "If cleanliness is next to godliness then we are indeed in Hell."

The captain, shaking from his fever, studied his carer

more closely as a call to prayer drifted in from a nearby minaret. Her crystalline eyes radiated intelligence and compassion; her wrists smelled of lavender. "I should probably ask your name," he pressed. "You seem to have me at a disadvantage."

"Clementine," she replied, her smile lighting up his soul. "Clementine Gresham."

Hugo noted her cut-glass accent and guessed that they moved in similar circles. Unbeknown to him, Clementine had already observed the captain as he slept. This was only to be expected as women of all ages tended to find him irresistible.

He was a handsome, virile man whose empire moustache was temporarily rendered less distinct by two weeks of beard growth. She had run her fingers along the blood-spattered uniform that hung by his bed, namely a black tunic patterned with gold braid, paired with scarlet trousers that seemed especially out of place in their dismal surroundings. Now that he was awake and chatting with her, Clementine imagined how dashing he must look in his finery. She saw he had the easy smile of someone who feels comfortable in their own skin and instantly thought him to be a charming, charismatic fellow.

Hugo Pinkerton lay back and resisted his fever. "Your name suits, does it not?" he croaked. "From the Latin word *clemens,* meaning mild or merciful. Are you going to be merciful to me, fair Clementine?"

"I am merciful to all of my patients, Captain Pinkerton. Now, if you will excuse me, I must attend to those poor souls who are in far greater need."

"Of course. Of course," he assented, feeling all at once guilty for his self-indulgence. "Perhaps you might revisit me from time to time?"

"Perhaps I might," she replied coyly. "Though Nurse Nightingale disapproves of her charges fraternising with patients."

"Quite so. And are you married, Clementine?" he grinned, pleased by his own boldness.

"I am not, Captain Pinkerton," she blushed. "Though it should be of no concern to you."

Meanwhile an infantryman had begun to shriek with pain as a surgeon struggled to cut the clothes from his mutilated body. Clementine rushed to assist, leaving Hugo alone to count his blessings.

*

Once his fever had subsided, Captain Pinkerton threw himself into efforts to improve the hospital's appalling insanitary conditions. Under Florence Nightingale's guidance, walls and floors were scrubbed with potash, fresh clothes and soaps were purchased locally and blankets replaced. Much to the relief of the beleaguered soldiers, a drainage team was sent by the British government to unblock the Turkish sewers that had failed to cope with an unsuppressed outbreak of dysentery. Despite being the entitled son of a baron and educated at Eton, Pinkerton saw much nobility in honest endeavour and took to his menial tasks with great gusto.

The officer encountered Clementine as he headed for the latrines with a bucket of soapy water in his good hand. "If my father could see me now," he remarked. "Perhaps you have found your true vocation, Captain," she quipped, arching her pretty eyebrows.

Seizing every opportunity to strike up a conversation with the object of his affection, Pinkerton set the pail on the floor and ran a sleeve across his grimy forehead. "I must say, Miss Gresham, that your Miss Nightingale is a hard taskmaster but I greatly admire her pluck."

Clementine leant in as if to divulge an unutterable secret. "She sees it as her calling from God, apparently."

"How wonderful!" the captain enthused. "The chaps will be comforted to learn that He and she are in direct communication."

*

Hugo shaved off his beard and each morning lit a candle for the purpose of waxing the tips of his splendid moustache. He took to wearing his uniform again and looked rather debonair as he dispensed beef tea to men who were bandaged to such an extent that they resembled a line of Egyptian mummies. On his final day, the captain was somewhat sad to leave and, wishing to introduce some levity to the occasion, boosted the soldiers' morale by leading them in a rousing sing-song.

"We shall miss you, sir!" shouted a blinded infantryman from his bed.

"And I shall miss every last one of you too," the captain replied, ceremoniously. "For I have yet to meet a finer body of men."

*

The Turks moored a small boat in the harbour, ready to ferry him to Constantinople. Thereafter a steamer would transport him to Marseille. Pinkerton sought out Clementine, hoping that she might agree to meet up with him back in England. He found her outside in the courtyard, flush-faced and dabbing her eyes with a handkerchief. "My dear Miss Gresham, what ails you?"

"Oh, I had hoped you wouldn't see me like this, Captain Pinkerton. I must look a frightful mess."

"Not at all. And I believe it was da Vinci who said that one's tears come from the heart and not from the brain."

At this, Clementine erupted in a convulsion of sobs and turned away from him through acute embarrassment.

Pinkerton wanted to wrap his arms around her but propriety stopped him from doing so. "My dear Clementine, what has brought this upon you?"

The nurse bared her wet face, emboldened by the need for clarity. "It's you, Hugo. Or rather the horrid thought that after today I may never see you again."

"I see," said Hugo, somewhat taken aback. "I wasn't at all aware that you held such feelings for me. Still, this makes what I am about to say so much easier. I was hoping that we might meet up once we are both returned to England."

"But to what end?" asked Clementine, her eyes reddened and lips trembling.

This seemed to Pinkerton to be the perfect moment. "You could call me an incurable romantic, sweet Clementine, but I hereby declare my love for you and very much hope that we might correspond with a view to marriage—"

The nurse was on the verge of collapse and leant against a wall for support. "But I am already betrothed to someone, Captain Pinkerton!" Her voice was shriller than she had intended it to be.

Pinkerton, not customarily lost for words, was temporarily dumbfounded. "Betrothed? But to whom?"

"You are certain to know him," she whimpered, wringing her hands. "Luther Hadley. Captain Luther Hadley—"

"Hadders, yes, of course. We trained together at the Royal Military Academy. A decent fellow, I recall."

"It was all so sudden," Clementine continued. "He was my suitor and all at once it seemed we were engaged to be married. I had barely the time to catch my breath."

"And where is Hadders now?" asked Hugo. "Last I heard, he saw battle at Alma."

"Indeed. He was wounded by rifle fire and taken from the battlefield in a cart. I had hoped to see him here in Scutari but, unbeknownst to me, he was on his way home whilst I was making the journey to Turkey."

"And his injuries? Were they life-threatening?"

The nurse looked skyward in an attempt to stem further tears. "No, not life-threatening although, as he lay wounded, he took a Russian sword to his face. I know no more than that as I've only received one letter from him thus far."

His plans dashed, Pinkerton put on a brave show. "Captain Hadley may have been unlucky in war but he has been most fortunate in love." He retrieved a piece of notepaper from his person that bore his address. "Please forget that I ever declared my love for you, Clementine. Your place is with your fiancé. All I ask is that we stay in touch as friends. I should love for us to meet up in more pleasant surroundings."

An officer called over, informing the captain that a carriage was ready to take him to the dock. Clementine was beside herself and at a loss for words. "Oh, Hugo—"

Pinkerton bowed at the waist and kissed her hand. "*Adieu,* Nurse Gresham. You will forever remain in my heart."

As he walked to his carriage, Hugo heard Clementine dissolve into tears behind him. He dared not look back for fear of precipitating his own.

*

After travelling overland through France, Captain Pinkerton reached Calais where he boarded a British navy clipper which set sail for England.

*

One of the curiosities of war is that the men who

survive it unscathed are often the ones who revel in its unspeakable horror the most. And this was the case at Pinkerton's parents' house where his father's friends, some of them veterans of the Battle of Waterloo, relived past glories over a sumptuous dinner.

"So tell us, young Hugo," blustered Lord Gudgeon, filling his port glass for the tenth time. "How many of those worthless Ruskies did you dispatch with that sabre of yours?"

The captain, who was rather less militant than his esteemed dining companions, considered his answer. "I killed a great many, sir, but took no pleasure in doing so."

"Nonsense!" barked the lord, spitting morsels of unchewed pheasant as he did so. "There is a great deal of satisfaction to be had by taking the life of someone who is trying to take yours."

"Quite so," said Pinkerton senior. "And let us not forget that, apart from being a great swordsman, my son is reputed to be the finest shot in the British army."

The captain continued in his quest to dampen their belligerence. "With respect to my father, and to all of you present, I bear the Russian man no ill. A Stanislav has as much right to walk God's earth as does a Stanley."

As a succession of aristocratic jaws dropped, Hugo's mother, an intuitive woman, thought it judicious to intercede. "The important point to consider is that my son has done his duty for queen and country. So, with that in mind, I should like to make a toast in his honour."

She slid back her chair and stood to raise a glass. All of those in attendance did likewise. "To Hugo!" she exclaimed.

"To Hugo!" they cheered as one.

*

Captain Pinkerton's injury left him unable to ride whilst wielding a weapon, which led to his medical discharge from the cavalry. Harbouring feelings of great guilt, Hugo was restored to the lap of luxury to which he had been accustomed previously. He resided in a roomy townhouse in Oxford and retained the services of his valet and housekeeper, both of whom had served him in the years between him finishing university and setting off to war. His valet, Edgar Pike, was a tall, inquisitive fellow notable for his unflappable air and immaculate appearance. His housekeeper, Bertha Dobson, was a straightforward woman with reproachful eyes and a backside as wide as a bathtub.

Within a year, the war was all but over. The Russian army, having suffered a terrible loss of men, had evacuated Sebastopol and was ready to capitulate. This precipitated battle-scarred British soldiers being allowed to return home in ever-increasing numbers. The captain, not wanting to allow his slight disability to get in the way of his horsemanship, learned to ride at a gallop with the reins looped in one hand.

*

Pinkerton, warmed by a roaring fire, was sitting in a leather wing armchair reading a copy of *Hard Times,* Charles Dickens' latest novel, when his valet stole into the drawing room bearing a silver salver perched on white-gloved fingertips. "Your newspaper, sir," Pike announced.

"Capital, my dear Pike. I am almost certain, you rogue, that you will have read it from first page to last before bringing it to me, so please regale me with one of its crowning moments."

Pike set down the salver and relayed the feature that had most interested him. "Well, sir, extraordinary as it might seem, the Americans are working on a voice communication device—"

Captain Pinkerton's eyebrows shot to the top of his forehead. "A voice communication device, Pike? What the deuce?"

"Yes, sir. They say that it will sit in one's home, sir, and will allow the purchaser to converse with a person of their acquaintance without having to be anywhere near them."

"My dear fellow, once we allow such a contraption into our homes the art of writing letters will be lost and people won't feel the need to venture outside."

"I sense that you don't approve, sir."

"I do not, Pike. I have the deepest affection for face-to-face social interaction and do not wish to spend my days blathering into a voice communication device."

"Then this should restore you to good cheer, sir. I present you with an envelope that bears your name and address, sir. Written by a lady's fair hand, it would appear."

A broad smile graced Pinkerton's handsome face, causing the tips of his moustache to point to opposite corners of the ceiling. He held the envelope in his good hand and studied the copperplate handwriting. The postmark showed that it was from London. "Would it have crossed your mind, Mr Pike, to have steamed open this envelope before reading its contents and resealing it?" asked Hugo with a glint in his eye.

"Certainly not, sir," replied the valet, pretending to be offended.

Pinning the envelope to his writing desk under the stump of his left hand, the captain sliced it undone with a silver letter opener.

"Mmmm, perfumed too," smiled Hugo, holding it to his nose.

"Honeysuckle, if I'm not mistaken, sir," said Pike impishly.

"That will be all for now, Pike. And thank you."

"My pleasure, sir," replied the valet, bowing courteously before exiting the room.

The correspondence comprised of one sheet of paper. Rather than beginning where one is supposed to, Pinkerton's eyes raced to the bottom of the page as he hoped to see Clementine's name there. And indeed it was! A name as dear to him as life itself, underscored with an Elizabethan flourish and prefixed with 'yours affectionately'. His heart was beating out of his chest as he began to read…

26, Bathsheba Place
Belgravia
London
October 19ᵗʰ, 1855

My dear Hugo,

I hope that this letter finds you in very good health and happiness. Barely a day passes without me reliving the sadness I felt upon watching you leave the hospital in Scutari. My emotions were rather mixed that day. In one way, I was relieved to see you removed from the squalor of that hellish place; in another, I missed you terribly from the first moment and wished you could stay. You might think me a sentimental fool but I began to understand fully Juliet's sweet sorrow at witnessing Romeo's departure, and I have not been able to hear that line thereafter without being reminded of our own moment in time.

It might not surprise you to learn that, shortly after you left for Marseille, I contracted cholera and very nearly perished from the disease. But for the endeavour of Nurse Nightingale and the grace of God, I would not be alive to write to you this day.

I am still to be married to Captain Hadley. He is much changed because of the war but remains a dependable sort. I am under strict instructions from both my parents to marry him and I staunchly intend to fulfil my duty.

As it may be my last opportunity to see you again, I

should like to invite you to a winter ball that is to be held at my parents' house here in Belgravia, in one month's time on the 19th of November. The official invitation is to be posted separately by a member of our household staff.

Could I entreat you to respond only in a formal manner? I fear that persons other than myself might intercept your correspondence.

Dear Hugo, it would gladden my weary heart to see you again, even if only for one evening. I shall never cease to remember your radiant smile in the gloomiest of surroundings.

Yours affectionately,
Clementine

*

On the night of the ball, the black horse clip-clopped to a halt, its smoky breath caught in the glow of a gas street lamp. Captain Pinkerton paid the driver of his hansom cab and stepped onto Belgravia's frosty cobble-stones wearing a dress coat to keep off the chill. The rest of his outfit incorporated a top hat and tails finished off with a fashionable cravat.

"My good fellow, may I feed your horse a carrot before you head off into the night?" asked the captain.

"Of course, sir. My 'orse loves a carrot, he does. I can't believe, sir, that a gent such as you would 'ave a bloomin' carrot in 'is pocket."

"My friend, it is a firm belief of mine that if a

gentleman is to secure the services of a London cab then he should certainly carry a carrot on his person. Why only tip the driver and not the horse?"

With the carrot consumed directly from Hugo's gloved hand, the driver bade him a good evening and, with a flick of his reins, clattered down the road.

The captain had purposely arrived late, knowing that a high-spirited crowd would help to mitigate any awkwardness between himself and Clementine's fiancé. A footman stationed at the door checked Hugo's invitation before helping him out of his coat. Engaging in small talk, the captain removed his top hat and laid his gloves inside before handing it to the manservant. With flawless synchronisation, he was received by another member of the household staff who escorted him along several corridors towards a babble of conversation and laughter.

A commodious, high-ceilinged drawing room had been cleared to reveal a floor space capable of accommodating sixty guests. The party was in full swing and Pinkerton was pleased to behold an atmosphere of high spirits and gaiety. He stood at the threshold with his arms clasped behind his back as his full name and rank were hollered out by the same servant who had shepherded him through the house.

After a succession of Chinese whispers, news of the captain's arrival reached the ears of Clementine, who lifted her crinoline dress from the parquet floor and swished excitedly through the chattering throng to greet him. Hugo saw her surface from a river of people, her long white gloves and slender arms lending her a swan-like quality. All else faded into the background as he was once more beguiled by her beauty. He was as much in love with her as ever.

Clementine was equally thrown by the captain's striking magnetism and became almost tongue-tied on her approach. "Dear Hugo, it is wonderful to see you. I so hoped you would come."

Pinkerton bowed at the waist and kissed the back of her gloved hand. "An ambush of tigers could not have kept me away, dear Clementine."

They stopped to share a moment, their eyes expressing what could not be said. Clementine was left fumbling for words. "Your hand seems fully healed, I notice."

"You are too kind," Hugo grinned. "Though it resembles more a knee than a hand."

"And has your impairment stopped you indulging in your passion for horse riding?"

"Not one bit, my dear Clementine," he replied. "Would a cat cease climbing trees just because it was missing its whiskers? Would a gorilla stop beating its chest just because it had lost a few teeth?"

Clementine chuckled at his wit. "I see that you have lost none of your charm, Captain Pinkerton. I have sorely missed your positivity in the face of adversity."

The officer smoothed his moustache. "You honour me, Miss Gresham. A gentleman goes in search of flattery as keenly as a bee hunts for pollen."

A sudden sadness clouded Clementine's face and she nervously scanned the room to see if her fiancé was within earshot. "How is it, Hugo, that you remain so buoyant after surviving the monstrosity of war, yet Luther is decidedly less so?"

Pinkerton adopted a more pensive tone. "No two chaps are the same, Clementine. Sadly, there are men in this world who would gaze upon a field of daffodils and see only the nettles."

"Indeed, but Luther is very much changed by war. He has become sharp and argumentative. His parents inform me that he has the most terrible nightmares and wakes the house screaming. I am at a loss as to what I should do."

"I feel for the poor fellow, Clementine," Hugo deliberated. "War leaves its mark on all of us. I am inclined to think that the elixir of time will soothe his suffering and that your union will go from strength to strength."

Clementine glanced over her shoulder, her anxiety deepening. "You may feel differently when you meet him, Hugo. He is not the same man you knew before."

"Then let us find him that I may see for myself," Pinkerton enthused, casting a raffish smile that caused Clementine to go weak at the knees. "I do know that he is marrying the most wonderful lady in the entire kingdom."

"I would beseech you not to say such things in his presence, dear Hugo. And please don't mention his dreadful scar. He is rather touchy about it."

"My lips are sealed."

*

They found Captain Hadley, resplendent in dress uniform, chatting with two other soldiers. Clementine stood Hugo to one side and courteously attracted her fiancé's attention above the rise and fall of violins being played. "Luther, might I steal you away from your companions for a short while? You will of course remember Captain Hugo Pinkerton from the military academy—"

Pinkerton wasn't quite prepared for the vibrant scar that ran from Hadley's forehead to the point of his chin, passing through his nose as it did so. Other than that, the fellow was recognisable by his russet hair and moustache – a human incarnation of a fox, Hugo had always thought.

"By George!" cried Hadley, stepping forward with a limp. "Clementine said that you might be coming and here you are, as devilishly handsome as ever!"

"It's an honour to see you again, Hadders," said Hugo warmly as they shook hands. "May I congratulate you on your impending marriage to Miss Gresham?"

Hugo saw instantly that his former cohort's smile was counterfeit and that something was amiss.

"Come, come, Pinkerton," Hadley tutted. "No need to be so formal. I shall wager that you did not address my fiancée as 'Miss Gresham' when you were alone together in Turkey."

"I fail to understand your drift, sir," Hugo replied, furrowing his brow.

Clementine was mortified. "Please, darling, don't—"

Her fiancé continued as if she were invisible. "And

how is it, sir, that some of us have put our lives on the line for queen and country while you have escaped with little more than a flesh wound?"

Pinkerton held Hadley's demonic gaze and noticed a misalignment of each side of the man's nose where it had been cloven in two and stitched back together again. "Perhaps I was lucky," replied Hugo, not wishing to get into an argument, knowing that the fellow's battle scars ran deeper than just the physical ones.

"Some might call it cowardice, sir," snarled the wounded fox. "I led my men from the front, Captain Pinkerton. From the front, sir."

"It would also appear that you led with your face," quipped Pinkerton, not able to stop himself.

"Damn you, sir!" cursed Hadley. "I shall take leave of you now but you are not to correspond with my fiancée again. Do you understand?"

Pinkerton bowed modestly. "I understand perfectly, sir."

Without delay, Captain Hadley returned to his friends leaving his fiancée and Pinkerton dumbfounded.

"It's probably best that I leave," said Hugo, maintaining a decorous distance between himself and Clementine.

"Now you see what has become of my betrothed," she sputtered. "Oh, Hugo, I am ashamed beyond measure."

"Allow the poor fellow time, Clementine. Just as every cloud has a silver lining, so each person has a saving grace. And that being said, I really must bid you *adieu*."

"Then please at least allow me the honour of seeing you to the door."

"Of course."

Clementine melted into the throng and Hugo followed her through the house until they reached the grand hallway. No one else was present, save for the footman who was by the front door and looking out onto the street.

Head bowed, Clementine was wringing her hands again, just as she had when they last parted. "My dear Hugo, because I knew I would be seeing you again, I eagerly awaited this night—"

Before she could utter another word, Pinkerton had smothered her with a kiss so passionate that she immediately lost all sense of time and place. Unbeknown to them, a female guest, who had stepped into the hallway from the library, withdrew immediately upon seeing their illicit kiss.

Regaining her capacity to think, Clementine stepped back from the captain whilst ardently wishing she could remain in his arms. "Oh dearest Hugo, we must not. We should not—"

"I understand," he replied, running a thumb across her tears and arriving at the realisation that he should place his true love's wishes before his own. "I wish you all the happiness in the world, my sweet Clementine, but please keep a place in your heart for me." Then, feeling a sense of déjà vu, he bowed at the waist and bade her farewell for the final time.

As Clementine sobbed quietly into a silk handkerchief, Captain Hadley's mother remained in the library, agonising as to whether she should reveal the details of what she had just witnessed to her son.

*

On his first day back from London, Captain Pinkerton's housekeeper was trying to ascertain why her master was off his food. "You normally have such a healthy appetite, sir. It ain't proper to eat nuffink after such a journey like what you just had."

"Trust me, I'm fine, Mrs Dobson. And I am most grateful for your kind concern."

"Not even some of me cock-a-leekie soup, sir?"

Hugo raised a smile. "No, not even some of your cock-a-leekie soup, Mrs Dobson."

"When a man is off his food there's usually a blinking woman involved, sir."

"Is that so?"

"It is so. And let me tell you something about us women for free, sir. A woman is like an ocean, sir, beautiful to look at but dangerous to cross."

"I shall bear that in mind, Mrs Dobson."

There was a sharp rat-a-tat at the front door and Pike headed downstairs to answer it. Almost as soon as the door was opened Pinkerton heard a strident voice, one he immediately recognised, polluting the quietude.

Mrs Dobson's expression was a mixture of astonishment and annoyance. "Blimey, who the blazes is that, sir?"

"Nothing for you to worry about, Mrs Dobson. Return to your duties and I'll see to it."

Pinkerton tidied his cravat and hastened down the

stairs. Upon reaching the hallway he was confronted by the sight of Captain Hadley ranting like a madman, his vulpine face as red as his scar.

Despite being in the eye of the storm, Pike remained unflappable. "There is a gentleman to see you, sir," he said dryly.

Hadley swaggered further forward. Behind him, but keeping a respectful distance, was his footman. "Pinkerton! You, sir, are a cad and an utter bastard!" fumed the interloper, brandishing a pair of leather gloves in Hugo's direction.

"Shall I fetch my rifle, sir?" Pike enquired.

"That won't be necessary," Hugo replied.

"Kissing a fellow officer's fiancée, sir!" Hadley bellowed, his eyes like hot coals. "Witnessed by my own mother, you despicable cur!"

Before Pinkerton could respond, Hadley slapped him hard about his face with the gloves. "To preserve my honour I demand satisfaction, sir! Pistols at dawn, sir!"

Pike sprang into action and set off hastily for the gun cabinet.

Hugo remained calm. He realised just how tormented his aggressor had become and how much the war had taken its toll on the wretched fellow. "Come, my dear Luther. Pistols at dawn, indeed! Let us take tea together in my drawing room where we will discuss this responsibly. I shall call upon Mrs Dobson to provide sandwiches."

Hadley slapped Pinkerton hard across the face again. "I would sooner eat my boots than drink tea with you, Pinkerton. Unless you wish to lose face, we shall meet at dawn on the heath yonder. Our servants shall act as our seconds. All you are required to do is to arrive with your service revolver."

Pike returned, carrying a loaded rifle. "I have not the faintest idea who you are, sir, but Captain Pinkerton is the finest shot in the country. You are unquestionably sentencing yourself to death."

"Ah, but a real man shows his true mettle under pressure," sneered Hadley. "I am firm in my belief that your master will not be able to shoot so well when his hand is shaking through fear."

"Poppycock!" retorted Pike. "Captain Pinkerton has been cited for extreme valour at the Battle of Balaclava. Queen Victoria herself is to award him a medal for gallantry."

Hadley's face twitched, his fox-like features never more pronounced.

Pinkerton's heart was filled with sorrow for the poor man, knowing that he wasn't of sound mind. "What purpose will this serve?" he beseeched, addressing his antagonist. "Should you win this duel, you will then face the rope, sir. There is no honour in two meaningless deaths, Luther."

A sly smile crept across Hadley's face. "My attendant is a military man, and I can see by the way he carries himself that yours is too. The duel is to take place in a copse at the break of dawn. The loser will be buried deep in the ground where he falls, and no one shall ever speak of it."

As a matter of honour, and seeing no escape, Pinkerton

accepted the challenge.

*

After a fitful night's sleep, Captain Pinkerton and his valet arrived at the heath on horseback. Waiting to receive them in front of a wintry thicket of trees were Captain Hadley and his grim-faced footman. A smoky mist hung low to the ground and the rising sun had planted pink clouds for those lucky enough to witness their beauty.

Pinkerton brought his steed to a halt and surveyed the scene before him. "How wonderful a day this is, Pike," he remarked. "Listen to the birds as they herald the morning. It is an insult to Mother Nature that one of us shall not see another like it."

"Good day, Pinkerton!" his opponent shouted. "I had half a mind that you would not show."

"On the contrary, I will always step forward when my honour is in question," Hugo replied.

Once they had dismounted, Pike tethered his and Captain Pinkerton's horses to a tree and indicated to Hadley's footman that he had brought a spade. Hadley was no longer wrathful in his disposition and even engaged his adversary in casual conversation as they strolled into the copse. "This is as good a place as any," he declared as they reached a clearing. "What say you, Pinkerton?"

Hugo had a calm authority about him. "I say no time like the present, Hadley. And may the best man win."

Pike, who had every confidence that his master would be the last man standing, provided Hugo with his Beaumont-Adams service revolver. "Good luck, sir," he said with an assured nod.

Hadley, dressed in full military finery, orchestrated proceedings. "We shall stand back to back, Pinkerton. On one of our attendants giving the command to begin we shall each walk ten paces, at which point we shall turn and fire. Just one shot and no more. Are you in agreement, sir?"

"I am, sir," replied Pinkerton. "And let whosoever wins this duel go on to live the lives of two men."

Hadley stepped forward, his coppery hair burnished gold by the low morning sun as it poured through the bare trees. "Then let us commence, sir."

The combatants stood back to back while their seconds agreed on who should issue the start command. Songbirds continued to chorus and Pike positioned himself so that he faced both duellists. "Advance!" he bellowed.

Each man strode forward solemnly. On his ninth pace, Pinkerton inhaled the cold air as if it were the sweetest perfume. On his tenth, he turned. Both men were now a fair distance apart and stood in a sideways-facing stance, each with his non-shooting arm tucked behind his back. The trees looked on indifferently.

Pinkerton watched Hadley raise his revolver and chose not to aim his own. "O Lord, let her be the last whisper in my ear," he muttered to himself as he prepared to meet his death.

Hadley's finger began to squeeze the trigger while Pike, aghast at his master's suicidal passivity, almost felt compelled to cry out.

Captain Hadley's hand began to shake violently. "Why do you not aim your weapon, sir?" he hollered.

"You have me at your mercy, Hadley," shouted Pinkerton. "For the love of God and for the sake of your future marriage, just shoot, damn you!"

Instead, Hadley hung his firearm by his knee and marched briskly forward. "The love you have for Clementine is so great that you are prepared to forfeit your life, Pinkerton?"

"I am incurably in love with her, sir," Hugo replied. "But her happiness is reliant on me not being around. So kill me now, sir, that I may one day love her in the afterlife."

Tears began to stream down Hadley's scarred face as he studied Pinkerton intently. "You were always the better man, Hugo. I have seen for myself the love in Clementine's eyes when she talks about you. Look at what is left of me, sir. How could she ever be happy?"

"In the fullness of time she will be, Hadley. I wish it with all of my heart."

"You are a good man, Pinkerton, and I am a mere shadow of what I once was. I did not want to believe it but now know it to be true. Clementine would be far happier with you—"

"Not so," said Pinkerton, seeing before him a broken man.

Hadley lifted his reddened eyes to the sky and studied

it, as if trying to remember its magnificence for eternity. He straightened himself and looked directly at his rival, remembering how good life had been when they were young cadets. "In the presence of these two witnesses, I want you to know that you have my full blessing, sir."

Before Pinkerton could stop him, his erstwhile friend put the revolver to his own temple and squeezed the trigger.

As a shot rang out, the horses bucked and birds took flight. Captain Luther Hadley crumpled to the ground, peaceful in death on a bed of frost-crisped leaves.

The Concubine and the Postman

Jaadoosthan, 1932

During the days of the British Raj, and before the outbreak of WWII, a concubine of extraordinary beauty, the maharaja's favourite, lived a life of unrivalled entitlement and security. She went by the name of Yara, meaning 'Little Butterfly' and, once seen, no man could fail to be enthralled by her. In fact, on one of his visits to the palace a British emissary remarked to the maharaja that Venus herself could not have been more enchanting.

As well as having a body that hardened penises and brought men galloping from their deathbeds, she was blessed with magical powers bestowed on her by Kali, the benevolent-but-wrathful Hindu goddess. She was supremely skilled in the art of seduction and able to bring her master to sexual release with consummate ease. The maharaja, to the envy of every red-blooded male in the region, remained the only man to have ever sampled her erotic delights.

Whenever she was able Yara Guneta liked to return to Bhula Diya, the wretched small town in which she was raised, and she was free to do so whenever His Highness was away on royal business. So neglected was her grotty hometown that even plagues thought to give it a miss. Furthermore, even though the royal palace was a mere ten miles away, the citizens had only seen their ruler once, this being the time he hurtled through in a Rolls Royce Phantom that had previously belonged to Marlene Dietrich.

Because she had captured the Maharaja's heart, no man dared lay a hand on Yara, knowing full well that if they did so they would be dipped up to their waists into cauldrons of boiling oil by the palace guards – a fate you wouldn't wish upon your worst enemy. Consequently she was able to stroll through the dusty streets of Bhula Diya entirely untroubled and was afforded a deference usually reserved for princesses. It wasn't at all unusual for sun parasols to be held above her head by reverential admirers, or for garlands of jasmine to be hung lovingly around her graceful neck.

Though Yara possessed shapeshifting skills and a whole host of mystical powers, she was happy with the cards she'd been dealt and chose not to use them aimlessly. The maharaja, despite being a fearsome man, was extremely kind to her and life in his royal palace was comfortable beyond her wildest dreams.

"My little butterfly has never forgotten her humble origins," her toothless mother Deepa would say routinely with unrestrained pride. "That sweet girl of mine is as modest now as when she was a child."

Everyone agreed and, out of politeness, purposely

neglected to remind Deepa of the time her sorceress daughter had turned an itinerant snake charmer into a rat after he had tried to slip his hand into her sari. His snake, not believing its sudden good fortune, struck out hard and fast and swallowed its master whole in one ravenous gulp.

Also consigned to local folklore was the time that Yara saw Ramesh the loan shark steal money from the begging bowl of a sleeping leper. When she confronted him, he lied through his gold teeth and denied any wrongdoing. Such a blatant display of dishonesty proved to be the biggest mistake of his rotten life for Yara cast a spell on him that replaced his lying tongue with one the size of a giraffe's. He promptly left the district in disgrace with his hefty tongue hanging down to his waist. In the meantime the leper, who had remained asleep throughout the entirety of this astonishing incident, woke to find himself cured of his disabling disease.

*

Bhula Diya remained sluggishly indifferent to the outside world and, once the monsoon rains had passed, the town became as hot as a tandoor. On days like these the skies were cloudless and one could see the maharaja's palace shimmering in the distance, basking like a gigantic lizard. The heat was so incessant that it forced the monkeys to stay in their trees and, if anyone were to listen keenly, each of the neighbourhood's bone-dry buildings could be heard heaving the weariest of sighs.

It was on one such afternoon that three idiot thieves strolled into town. They were dressed simply in loincloths and shawls, each one as vile and as witless as the next. All three were wild-haired and bedraggled, as if they had just staggered from a fight to the death with a family of chimpanzees. Two were rake thin with knees wider than their legs; the other was a blubbery villain whose broad buttocks swayed like those of a departing elephant. They had walked for days carrying bundled belongings on their sweaty backs, hoping that this godforsaken place would prove an easy target for their unsophisticated brand of villainy.

The first person they came across was Jaideep Chowdhury, Bhula Diya's only postman. "Sahib!" shouted Sanjay, the more talkative of the two skinny thieves. "Where in this splendid place can three hungry fellows find some food?"

Jaideep, a kind, virtuous bachelor with timid eyes, was immediately suspicious of the three unshaven rogues. Despite his misgivings, however, he was predisposed to show hospitality to strangers so he leant his bicycle against a railing and pressed his palms together in polite salutation. "Sahibs, if you were to cross the river bridge over there you would immediately see Rishi's pakora stand. Most delicious they are, and also very reasonably priced."

The trio regarded the postman's crisp uniform with disdain and casually thanked him with a succession of grunts before trooping off in the direction he had indicated. Jaideep shook his head and followed the villains' knock-kneed progress with interest. "That large fellow has the backside of an elephant," he chuckled to himself.

While crossing the bridge, the three idiot thieves held a competition to see who could spit mucus furthest into the river; in due course Om, the elephant man, was declared their proud champion.

Kabir, the least talkative of the imbeciles, scratched his dirty crotch and directed a bony finger towards Rishi's food stall. "Look, there is a very sexy lady at the pakora stand. If we move quickly we could touch her up."

"That is a most excellent idea," replied Om, the human elephant. "And if we touch her up good, she might even pay for our pakoras."

"She might even buy us the whole damn stand if we were kind enough to screw her!" declared Sanjay with great optimism.

By the time they reached the food cart, the beautiful lady had departed leaving behind an aroma of perfume and scented oils.

Rishi the pakora man was busy cutting a cauliflower into florets when Sanjay addressed him. "*Namaste*, pakora-*wallah*. May I ask you who the very pretty lady was? The one with the expensive sari. Such a fancy type."

Rishi, whose toupée resembled a cowpat, noted the men's bundled belongings, which were held in cotton bedsheets. "Sahibs, you fellows are clearly new in town. That woman is tremendously famous in Bhula Diya and also much further afield. Her name is Yara and she is the most beautiful of all the maharaja's concubines—"

"Ahhh … concubines!" the three men chorused, repelling flies with their halitosis and nodding their heads sagely.

After a protracted and extremely awkward silence, Sanjay asked a question. "Please, Sahib, what is a concubine?" The other two leaned in for enlightenment, having also pretended to know what the word meant.

Rishi struggled to offer an answer. He felt it a breach of trust to talk about Yara in such an unseemly way to three complete strangers. "Friends, she is kept in the palace fundamentally to be of, um, *service* to His Excellency when his wife isn't available."

The three halfwits stared blankly back at him. He might just as well have tried to explain Newton's First Law of Motion to them. "Um, how can I put this plainly?" Rishi continued, dropping a freshly made pakora into the hot oil. "These ladies attend to His Highness's every need … his *every* need."

"Ah-ha!" chimed Sanjay, as the penny dropped. He then formed a circle with the thumb and forefinger of one hand and repeatedly poked an index finger through it so that his brainless friends would also latch on. Rishi rolled his eyes as the three morons cackled like mad witches.

"Look! A tiger!" shrieked Sanjay, hoping he could steal some pakoras while the vendor was distracted.

Rishi remained unmoved. He'd seen every sneaky trick in the book of chicanery several times over and fired a warning by belligerently chopping an aubergine in two with his large preparation knife. His sudden annoyance had almost sent his toupée into a spin. "Are any of you damn fools actually going to purchase anything? If not, clear off as I have much work to do."

"Hey, hold onto your hair, pakora-*wallah*," Sanjay countered. "Of course we will order from your mouth-watering selection."

After feasting on Rishi's pakoras, and having also stolen flyblown food offerings left in shrines for the gods, the crooked threesome found temporary rented accommodation in a mud-walled, tin-roofed habitation that was previously used as a cowshed.

"See! I told you fellows that we would soon be living the high life!" crowed Sanjay, his eyes as big as mangoes.

"If only our families could see us now!" marvelled Kabir.

"I cannot even believe our good fortune!" grinned Om, delighted to see three bamboo beds occupying the concrete floor.

Darkness and a million mosquitoes descended on Bhula Diya. The rickshaw men assembled under streetlamps; large fruit bats took to the sky and rabid dogs slept on cooled pavements. Inside their converted cowshed, the three idiot thieves were planning a night of burglary and took from their belongings a selection of cudgels, hammers, crowbars, screwdrivers and one large handsaw.

"Hey, hey, look!" Om shouted, his elephantine buttocks barely able to keep up with him. "The maharaja's pretty porcupine is right outside!"

"What is a porcupine?" asked Kabir, scratching his

head.

"The pakora-*wallah* already told you, you idiot. A young lady who does jiggy-jiggy with the maharajah. How will you ever educate yourself if you don't damn well listen?"

His cohorts gathered at a square hole in the wall that served as a window. Sure enough, only a short distance away and taking in the night air stood the maharaja's concubine contoured by moonlight and as beautiful as Mohini, the famous enchantress.

After they'd crowded the window and ogled her for a good two minutes, Sanjay was first to speak. "Brothers, an absolutely excellent opportunity has fallen into our laps—"

"How so?" chorused Om and Kabir.

"The maharaja would pay a lot of rupee for the safe return of his sexy fucky-fucky lady if we were to kidnap her."

"Oh my bloody God," enthused Om. "That is the greatest damn idea that you have ever had."

"Quite possibly the best bloody idea that any man has ever had!" exclaimed Kabir.

"And because of this we will be rich beyond our wildest dreams," continued Sanjay. "But, brothers, we must act bloody damn fast and strike like cobras."

*

Yara, who was staying at her mother's house nearby, was enjoying a meditative moon prayer salutation when Sanjay crept soundlessly behind her and put out her lights with one determined strike of his cudgel. Checking that the coast was clear, the men dragged her insensate body into their lair.

They lay her on the floor, her chic white sari decidedly at odds with the squalid surroundings. Sanjay poured a glug of chloroform onto a rag and held it over her nose and mouth. Yara roused before the chemical could take effect and started to struggle, so Om coshed her over the head again.

"You wouldn't think it to look at her but she's a fighter, this one," said Sanjay as the chloroform finally rendered her completely unconscious.

Om undid the drapes of Yara's sari and pulled up her *choli* to expose her breasts. "So very beautiful," he said, letting his hands wander. "Maybe we should have a little fun with her before we set out our demands, *na*?"

"Yes, she needs to be broken in, like a pair of new shoes," suggested Kabir.

"When was the last time you had new shoes?" scoffed Sanjay.

"When was the last time he had a woman?" Om smirked.

Weighing up their options while his accomplices circled poor Yara like ravenous hyenas, Sanjay arrived at a decision. "Brothers, listen. You both know me to be a man with very few morals—"

Om and Kabir nodded their heads in full agreement.

"—but I do draw the line at rape. And in any case, His High and Mightiness wouldn't want his prized possession back if she were spoiled in such a fashion."

The other two gazed down at their captive with a look of dismay on their unattractive faces.

Sanjay, keen to enthral them with his master plan, continued. "First, we tie her to a bed so she can't escape. Then, we cut off one ear and send it in a ransom note to the palace—"

"Who among us can write a note?" asked Om, shrugging his shoulders.

"I'm perfectly capable of writing a note," confirmed Sanjay. "They taught me to read and write in prison."

"You are indeed a very clever fellow," marvelled Kabir.

Without further ado, they tethered the concubine to one of the flea-ridden beds, administering more chloroform as she began to groan. After removing her bangles, they cut the rings from her toes.

"Be careful to take only one earring, my brothers," Sanjay instructed.

"Have you gone bloody mad?" remarked Om. "They look jolly damn expensive!"

"Yes, but how will the maharaja be able to tell her ear from anyone else's unless the earring is still attached?"

"See? What am I always telling you, Kabir? Our Sanjay is a bloody genius," Om chirped.

"Without him, we wouldn't be half as successful," Kabir said with deference.

"And this fancy-pants maharaja will know we mean business," Sanjay added.

They heated a knife in the flame of a candle and proceeded to cut off one of Yara's ears. Smoke rose from the blade and the men giggled like children.

"Smells like tandoori chicken," Kabir ventured, licking his lips.

Suddenly, as if woken from the grave, Yara opened her eyes and screamed like a banshee.

"Bloody damn shit!" blustered Sanjay. "Quick, bash her over the head!"

Om coshed her sturdily on the temple but she sat up, unaffected, and strained at her ropes. "Who the hell are you to harm me?" she blazed, her words carrying venom. "The maharaja has had men's eyelids sewn together just for staring at me. You imbeciles will rue the day you thought to lay a finger on me!"

"Ha! This coming from a woman who is tied to a bed and missing one ear," chuckled Sanjay.

To keep her quiet, Om whacked her across the back of the head while Kabir pressed a chloroformed rag against her face. Unable to pass a curse under such circumstances, Yara slipped into a state of deep unconsciousness.

"You damn fool, Kabir!" stormed Sanjay. "You have given her enough chemical to put a bloody buffalo to sleep!"

"She was shouting about sewing our eyelids together," grumbled Kabir.

"Oh, bloody God! She has no pulse!" Om bleated, pressing his sausage fingers to her neck.

"Bloody damn, no!" cursed Sanjay. "A mongoose would make a better kidnapper than either of you two!"

"So, what do we do now?" whined Kabir.

"The plan still goes ahead," Sanjay continued, his eyes

suddenly as wise as Aristotle's. "We post the ear to the palace, along with our demands. We also tell them that if they're stupid enough to set a trap, we will kill her."

"But we *have* killed her," declared Om.

"Yes, you idiot! But the maharaja doesn't know that, does he?"

"Genius!" shouted Kabir.

*

Later, while the locals slept, they fished an envelope from the town's one and only post box using a long metal spike. After crossing out the envelope's address and its written contents, Sanjay scrawled a ransom note that was intended to galvanise the maharaja into immediate action. Yara's ear, along with its earring, was placed inside the envelope and, before dawn's first chorus, her body was buried in a coconut grove on the outskirts of the town.

Unbeknown to the three cretinous thieves, Yara was still very much alive. Upon regaining consciousness she cast a terrible curse on the men for their cruelty. Then, with only dirt to breathe, she died almost immediately.

*

The villains, certain in their belief that a life of pampered luxury would soon be theirs, trooped back to their humble abode with triumphant smiles on their unpleasant faces.

Sanjay was scratching the sweat from his balls when all at once his scrotum, along with its testicular contents, completely disappeared. Just as he was trying to come to terms with this alarming development, his penis vanished also. "Waaaah! Waaaah!" he shrieked pulling his loincloth down and jumping about as if bullets were being fired at his feet.

"What is it, Sanjay?" Om asked. "Why all the bloody screaming?"

"Look! Look! Waaaah!" he shrilled. A neat cavity had taken the place of his manhood.

Om was utterly astonished. "Since when did you have a *punani*, Sanjay? I'd keep that quiet if I were you." No sooner had he said this than his own meat and two veg also vanished into thin air. Simultaneously Kabir suffered the same unnerving predicament. As one, they howled like drowning sailors while the morning sun rose in the sky.

Worse was to follow. As Yara's curse continued to evolve, the villains' skin began to char and their bones started to break. Their terrible screams sent cockroaches scuttling into storm drains and rats up drainpipes. Soon all that was left of the three idiot thieves was a putrid pile of ash.

*

Jaideep Chowdhury had just begun his postal round when Yara's mother ran to him, a look of distress erupting from her toothless face. "Jaideep! Jaideep!

Have you seen my beautiful Yara?"

"No, I'm afraid not Deepa-*ji*. Why? What on earth has happened?"

Deepa was frantic; she'd spent the entire night searching for her daughter. "Oh, Jaideep, I am so terribly worried. She stepped outside in the late evening to take in the night air and hasn't returned home since."

"Perhaps she was unexpectedly called back to the palace by His Majesty and didn't have time to say goodbye?" ventured the postman, hoping to ease her concern.

"No, she would never leave without telling me," Deepa whimpered. "Something most terrible has happened to my baby. I can feel it in my bones."

Despite wanting to join in the hunt for Deepa's missing daughter, Jaideep felt that this would be a dereliction of duty and so he continued his round while the townsfolk organised themselves into separate search parties. As he rode his bicycle he allowed himself a bygone memory, the one where, as children, he walked Yara home from school. After checking that no one could see them, she had asked him for a secret kiss but, out of propriety, he flatly refused. *What was I thinking?* he thought, bitterly regretting missing out on such a beautiful chance. Though she didn't know it, Yara was the sole reason he had remained a bachelor. He worshipped her from afar and loved no other.

Upon unlocking the post box, one envelope stood out among the rest: a bloodstained one with its address crossed out. In place of the previous address were the words: *To his majistys pallice and not to be opunned by anywun else.* The envelope intrigued him. It bulged slightly and an analytical prod suggested it contained two mystery items. *Why the bloodstains?* he wondered. *And why is it addressed to the palace?*

Unfortunately, while he was considering this curious puzzle, a street dog padded up to him and, after one curious sniff, grabbed the envelope in its teeth. Jaideep tried to wrest it from the beast's jaws, whereupon the paper ripped, causing its grisly contents to land in the dust. Casting aside his shock, he snatched the ear before the hound could have it for breakfast.

With Yara's unexplained disappearance still uppermost in his mind, he read the note from the torn envelope with a sense of foreboding: *we hav kidnapt your girl. Put sootcase with one thousund rupees under banyan tree in villij senter and you will get her. No dam funny bisniss or she is ded.*

This presented him with an alarming dilemma. The maharaja, a deeply suspicious man, would most likely consider him to be involved in the kidnap plot if he were to turn up at the palace with a bloodstained envelope and its contents. Then there was Yara's mother to consider; didn't she deserve to be told about her daughter's kidnap?

Fearful for his life, but also mindful of doing the right thing by Deepa and safeguarding Yara, Jaideep wrapped the earringed ear in a handkerchief then cycled home. He placed it in the centre of his bed until he could figure out his best course of action.

*

By the time he had finished his shift, Jaideep had decided to put ethics before self-preservation and resolved to bring the ransom note and severed ear round to Deepa's house.

Arriving home, he was unsettled by a grunting noise emanating from his bedroom. Fearful that the three scoundrels might be ransacking his house, he grabbed a cricket bat for protection.

He opened the bedroom door and the scene that befell him turned his blood to ice. Yara's head had grown back from her severed ear – but minus her beautiful eyes.

"Get away from me, you vile bastards!" she yelled, her hollow eye sockets searching blindly for the sight they had once possessed. Her sorceress powers had not yet returned to her and her detached head wobbled helplessly in the centre of the bed.

Jaideep, though deeply unnerved to behold such a terrifying sight, sought to reassure her. "Yara, relax. It's me, Jaideep the postman—"

"Please don't tell me you are involved with those jackals, Jaideep," her pretty mouth responded. "You, one of my dearest friends!"

"Of course not," he assured her, perturbed to be holding a conversation with a talking head that was minus its eyes. "I don't know where to begin... I found your ear inside an envelope that also contained a ransom note. I panicked and brought it home until I could think what to do for the best."

Yara's beautiful brown eyes popped back into her skull and a smile returned to her glossy lips. "Aww, so sweet,

Jaideep. You always were thoughtful and kind."

"You really think so? I felt such a coward for not reporting it immediately. I was terrified of what the palace guards might do to me. In reality, I acted with dishonour."

"You forget that I've know you since you were a shy schoolboy, Jaideep. Even then you acted with honour. I don't suppose you remember but I once asked you to kiss me."

Jaideep blushed. "I do remember."

Yara's talking head continued in a honeyed voice. "You are never far from my thoughts, Jaideep. Even when I am alone with His Highness, it is you I make love to."

Wonderstruck by this revelation, Jaideep opened his heart. "Oh, Yara. I never knew you felt this way. I have always loved you. Only you."

"So, kiss me now," Yara's head urged, her eyes blazing with desire.

Jaideep was too fearful. "But His Majest—"

"His Majesty isn't here, Jaideep," she interjected. "Please don't deny me that kiss. It's all I've ever wished for."

Almost deferentially, Jaideep leant over Yara's face. Her smile encouraged him to shed his customary inhibitions and he kissed her tenderly on the lips. She tasted of coconut and cardamom.

As she returned his kiss with interest, Yara's neck and shoulders grew from her head, shortly followed by her lissom body clothed in the same white sari she had been buried in. All her jewellery was returned to her and, as she reached for him, a cluster of bangles slid down her elegant arms and rattled to a halt.

She sat up and looked him directly in the eye. "Jaideep, I am nearly thirty years old. The maharajah will soon tire of me and find a younger favourite. I know when the time comes that there will no longer be a life of luxury for me. Would you consider waiting for me, that we might one day live a happy life together?"

Tears formed in the corner of the postman's eyes and ran down his cheeks. "Yara, my love, I would happily wait an eternity for you."

Seized by a moment of inspiration Yara's eyes lit up and a playful smile adorned her beautiful face. "Could you come with me to see my mother? I have a most incredible idea—"

*

It didn't go unnoticed by the palace staff that the maharaja had become an obliging, more agreeable person these past few weeks. To add to their astonishment his wife had also taken a turn for the better, her imperiousness seemingly a thing of the past. The royal couple had become inseparable, as if their bodies had been taken over by much kinder people. The concubines were retained only as palace guests, not as playthings in a gilded prison.

And the most famous concubine of them all, Yara Guneta, was rumoured to have eloped with the local postman because neither were seen again.

Extinction

Hovering in mid-air outside the door to his spaceship, T'nera gazed out one last time upon his dying planet. Once its surface had become too hot to support liquid water, it was only a matter of time before its crops had failed and planet-wide stocks of drinking fluids had run dangerously low. As the most eminent scientist on Apromis, it had been decided that he alone would receive a thrice-daily ration of the planet's last dregs of drinking water, dispensed by a military android programmed to self-destruct once the controllers were no longer able to control it.

Vaguely humanoid in form save for an exoskeleton and owlish eyes, T'nera remained levitated outside the door to his spaceship, his binocular vision registering the extinction of an advanced civilisation. Powerless to stop even his wife and children dying from thirst, he'd continued his research in his laboratory even though he knew that a last-ditch fix was impossible to achieve.

With a precious cargo of embryos held in cryonic suspension pods and a crushing sadness in his soul, Apromis's only surviving inhabitant closed the hatches and steeled himself for a mission that was likely to fail. Fighting back tears, he set navigation coordinates for Planet Earth, a fertile rock in a different solar system known to be capable of supporting life.

*

The journey took almost two years longer than anticipated. By the time T'nera had passed Planet Earth's moon, almost all of his water provision was used up.

His craft penetrated Earth's atmosphere and aerobraked, transforming kinetic energy into thermal. Atmospheric friction caused the body of the scientist's spaceship to glow red hot as it entered the blue airspace above England, whereupon two American interceptor fighter jets were scrambled together with three British stealth fighter jets.

Activating an invisibility filter, T'nera transformed his ship into a rain cloud that was indistinguishable from others around it. Much to the fighter pilots' bewilderment, all evidence of an unidentified flying object promptly disappeared from their tracking radar.

From a height of 7,000 feet, and invisible to the naked eye having altered his solid body matter into gases, T'nera stepped from the cloud and floated towards the King George V Playing Field in Cambridge. The small measure of satisfaction he'd derived from getting this far was blighted by the realisation that Earth's air was having an asphyxiating effect on him. Short of breath and intolerant to the high levels of carbon dioxide, he glided through the doors of a birthing centre on the Addenbrooke Hospital site hoping to locate a purer supply of oxygen.

With time fast running out, and beginning to lose consciousness, T'nera realised he desperately needed to find a human host. He was very near to death when his heat haze coasted over the bare stomach of an expectant mother and entered her womb. Unbeknownst to her, Emily Morton's first baby was about to be born with the anatomy of an infant and the mindset of an alien.

"A bonny baby boy!" announced the midwife, prior to clamping the umbilical cord.

"A bonny baby boy," T'nera repeated under his breath, soft enough not be heard. Although he was thankful to be alive, this bizarre scenario was not one he had planned for.

*

Nine months passed. Apart from finding himself unable to control the alarming frequency with which foul-smelling waste products were discharged from his gastrointestinal tract, T'nera adapted to his new reality with more ease than he had anticipated.

It was of great concern to him that it was presently impossible to access the embryos on his stranded ship; he also had to live with the guilt of knowing that he'd stolen the unrealised personality of a human child.

His *de facto* parents, Emily and Jack, were considerate and attentive. They'd named him Luke and their unswerving adoration was equal to the love T'nera had lavished on his own children.

Realising the terrible shock this would bring upon Emily and Jack, T'nera decided not to articulate his thoughts and so refrained from speaking altogether. In his thirst for human knowledge, however, he had once climbed from his cot in the dead of night and memorised every word in the *Oxford English Dictionary*. More recently, he'd become accustomed to secretly using the internet to cultivate a better understanding of the world in which he was living. Other than this, and impeded by his underdeveloped body, he had no choice but to continue to rely on the ministration of his parents.

Though T'nera appreciated Emily and Jack's good intentions, their puerile baby talk continued to exasperate him and almost drove him to break his silence. They, in turn, were worried that he hadn't gurgled as much as a "Mama" or a "Dadda" by his first birthday. They shared their concerns with a health visitor who reassured them that this was perfectly normal.

*

Jack sensed that something was on Emily's mind when he returned home from work one evening. Ostensibly all seemed normal: a casserole was cooking in the oven and Luke was sitting in his highchair, contentedly feeding himself chopped banana with a plastic fork. Jack's wife, however, seemed curiously unsettled.

"Is everything OK, Emily?" he asked. "You look as if

you're dying to tell me something."

Emily beckoned him into the living room and stood there wringing her hands.

Jack knitted his brow and sought to comfort her. "Oh, Em, what on earth has happened?"

His wife remained dithery and glanced into the kitchen where their son held her gaze. "Come over here," she whispered, retreating further into the room as if she were about to divulge something of great importance. "Now, you're going to think that what I'm about to say is crazy but I'm just going to say it anyway—"

Jack was on tenterhooks and wondered why she was whispering when there was no one else around.

Emily drew a deep breath and continued. "It's about Luke. There's something very peculiar about him—"

"Peculiar?" Jack repeated, placing his hands on his hips. "Peculiar in what way?"

"Now, Jack, I don't want you to make fun of me or ridicule me. I just want you to hear me out."

"Yes, of course. I'm listening."

"OK, here goes… While Luke was sleeping in his cot I made use of the time to catch up on the ironing. So while he was upstairs having a nap, I ironed here in the living room with the TV on—"

Her husband listened intently and nodded at all the right moments as his wife continued. "With all the clothes folded, I crept upstairs so as not to wake him. There was a glow coming from the office. I kid you not, there he sat on piled-up cushions on a chair looking at the computer screen!"

Her whisper rose in volume at the end of her report and Jack noticed her eyes becoming wild He immediately sensed that the strain of motherhood was beginning to take its toll. "Emily, darling, I have no idea how he managed to clamber up onto the computer chair but even so, he probably just likes looking at the pretty pictures—"

"You're not listening to me," Emily hissed, exasperation rising in her tone. "He'd piled cushions on the chair so he could see over the desk. He was *using* the bloody mouse."

"Baby, just listen to what you're saying. This is madness—"

"Don't you patronise me, Jack. I know what I saw – and I haven't even got to the really freaky bit yet."

"Go on," said Jack, trying to appear sympathetic.

"Luke's whole demeanour changed when he noticed me. One second he was studying the computer screen, the next he was holding his arms out to me. It was almost as if the whole baby thing was an act."

Jack released a dispirited sigh. "Jesus, Em. How can a baby be anything other than a baby? You're reading far too much into this."

"OK, so how could he get onto the computer without the security pin? I always log out."

"Well, perhaps you left it switched on. I don't log out unless it's necessary. Christ, Em! He's a baby, for God's sake!"

"Keep your voice down, he's listening."

"What do you mean, he's listening? He hasn't the

faintest idea what we're talking about and I can speak as loud as I want!"

Emily looked towards the kitchen. Luke was sitting in his high chair gazing intently in their direction. In her estimation, he *appeared* to be listening. This spurred her on; she was determined that Jack would take her seriously. "Come upstairs with me. I'll show you something that will stop you in your tracks."

Jack's shoulders sagged. "Go on then," he grimaced and followed her up.

Emily leaned over the desk and clasped the mouse. "After I put him back in his cot, *this* is what I saw on the search history—"

Jack stood shoulder to shoulder with his wife and studied the topics that were listed: Theoretical Physics; Astronomy and Space Science; Bioengineering; Sustainability in Space; NASA Innovative Advanced Concepts; Eleven Top Science and Technology Research Labs…

"And your point is *what*, exactly?" he asked.

"My point, Jack, is that these weren't keyed in by me. I'm trying to present you with the facts but you're just not listening to me."

"I'm not listening to you because what you are suggesting is too ludicrous to be taken seriously. I'm worried about you, Emily. Could your mother maybe help out a couple of days a week?"

Emily lasered him a glare worthy of a Gorgon. Without saying another word, she brushed past her husband and headed downstairs to fix supper. He followed sheepishly.

Each time he tried to reason with her, she shot him down with a few 'talk-to the-hand' gestures.

Once in the kitchen, and fed up with his wife's sulk, Jack resorted to sarcasm by way of retaliation. "Hey, Luke. Listen up, son. Apparently, your mummy thinks that you are a scientific genius capable of mastering computers before you can even talk!"

Luke's unforeseen reply wiped the grin from his father's face. "I can indeed talk," he said, steepling his chubby little fingers.

Jack stepped back aghast, his jaw hanging like a horse's nosebag. Emily spun around and stared at her son in utter disbelief. A stunned silence ensued while Luke considered his opening statement.

"Please sit down," he urged finally, his crisp eloquence chillingly unnatural coming from a mouth bracketed by baby dimples. "I apologise for not speaking sooner but I knew it would be too much of a shock. For whatever reason, I was born with a superhuman intelligence. I thought it best to keep this to myself until the time was right. Perhaps this *is* the right time."

His parents sank to their seats in slow motion, their eyes wide at what they were witnessing.

Luke smoothed tufts of downy hair and placed his tiny hands on the high-chair's plastic tray as a single tear fell from his eye. "I understand that this is a lot to take in but I want you to know that I love you both *so* much and hope that this hasn't broken the close bond that we share."

With motherly instinct overriding her astonishment,

Emily sought to reassure her son and rushed to comfort him. "Oh Luke, I knew you were special, my darling little boy. We love you so, so much."

Jack, despite feeling as if he were having an out-of-body experience, joined his wife and kissed his baby's roseate cheeks. At that moment, without quite understanding why, he feared for their future happiness.

*

Although they tried to give their extraordinary son as normal a life as possible, Jack and Emily couldn't stem the tide of societal astonishment. Before he'd reached his second birthday, Luke had appeared on daytime TV shows and was even invited to be a guest speaker at The Cambridge Union debating society. His fame spread like wildfire; soon the entire world wanted to know about this infant whose intellect surpassed that of some of the world's leading mathematicians and scholars. He famously beat a chess grandmaster, who stormed off after their televised match claiming that the child must have been equipped with a hidden listening device, his moves being dictated to him by a rival chess champion seeking to humiliate the grandmaster.

The great and the good of the scientific world were beside themselves with excitement after reading Luke's written hypothesis about the building blocks and symphonic strings of the universe. The child's brilliance was 'out of this world', they chorused.

Such an unprecedented display of human intelligence

didn't go unnoticed by hawks in MI5 and the CIA. Without prior warning, the Morton family were visited by two genial British secret-service agents, one male and one female, who expounded on the bright future that Luke could have within their organisation.

"Mr and Mrs Morton, your son possesses the analytical skills that we look for and his intellect is unparalleled," explained the woman, as she eyed Luke with acute curiosity. "He would receive all the care and support he could possibly need and you, as parents, would be involved in all the day-to-day decisions about his welfare and development."

"You make it sound like a job interview," said Jack, uncertain as to what to do for the best.

"It is," the male agent replied. "Only Luke is a shoo-in. The job's his if he wants it. And, although this won't be your prime concern, you will all be financially secure for the rest of your lives."

"So, what do you say?" asked the female agent.

*

One month later, having signed a raft of legal documents, the Mortons were blindfolded and driven to a top-secret Ministry of Defence bunker built deep beneath the English countryside. Luke sat strapped into his car seat, his chubby little legs dangling, excited to learn more about the underground facility they were being taken to.

The bunker was a sprawling subterranean city with

reinforced walls capable of withstanding a nuclear attack. Once inside its vast confines, the family's blindfolds were removed and they were transported along seemingly endless corridors in a convoy of golf buggies.

Luke instantly felt at home in this environment. After passing a hospital and a gallery of shops, cafeterias and restaurants, he caught glimpses of control rooms with massive touchscreen walls that reminded him of the hologrammatic ones he'd left behind on Apromis.

Their buggy drew to a halt outside an edifice guarded by armed soldiers. The family knew the MI5 operatives only as Agent Alpha and Agent Beta. The female, Agent Alpha, spoke directly to Luke's parents. "As we've previously discussed, this is where you part company from your son while we run him through a series of aptitude tests. Agent Beta will take you for tea or coffee and give you the VIP tour." A thin smile appeared on her face.

After passing a retina scan allowing her access through a succession of sliding doors, Agent Alpha lifted Luke and carried him to a brightly-lit room that resembled an operating theatre.

Luke's enthusiasm vanished immediately. "Why have you brought me here?" he asked, peering over her shoulder at a contingent of physicians and surgeons who wore scrubs and surgical masks.

"Relax, Luke, we just need to take a blood test for our records, that's all," said Agent Alpha soothingly.

"No. I forbid it!" Luke shouted, squirming in her arms.

Agent Alpha nodded to the head surgeon who took Luke from her and laid him on an operating table where surgical assistants strapped him down. Beyond a one-way mirror stood a delegation of scientists alongside an American general, a British field marshal and a team of high-ranking secret-service operatives. While the child wriggled, crying out for his mother and father, blood was drawn from a vein. Shortly after, a general anaesthetic rendered T'nera, the last of his species, unconscious.

The facility boasted its own state-of-the art science laboratories and the results of the blood tests were later revealed to the command dignitaries as they sat around a boardroom table. A scientist, visibly excited by his findings, outlined them on a flipchart. "Whereas we would usually expect to find twenty-three pairs of chromosomes, we have identified twenty-six. The additional three pairs are not of a protein previously seen. Furthermore, we have found DNA not known in our science—"

"So what does that mean in straightforward terms?" asked the American general.

The scientist took a sharp intake of breath and prodded his spectacles. "Gentleman, we can only conclude that the subject is an extra-terrestrial."

Those in attendance gasped while Agent Alpha punched the air shouting, "I knew it!"

The British field marshal asked the scientist to leave the room so that the group could secretly discuss the ramifications of what they'd just heard.

Once the scientist had departed, the American general

was first to weigh in. "It goes without saying but not a word of this should reach the President or the Prime Minister. Are we all agreed?"

As one, the attendees nodded.

"Right, I'll start the ball rolling," said the field marshal. "Will this creature prove to be an asset or a danger?"

"He'd be a tremendous asset to us," ventured an MI5 commander.

"Yes, but we don't know where his allegiances lie or even what his mission is," a CIA executive argued. "In my opinion, the risks far outweigh any potential benefits."

"And what if the Russians were to get their hands on him?" added an MI5 agent.

A more pacifistic CIA operative shook his head, astonished by what he was hearing. "But think of all the scientific breakthroughs this little guy might be capable of. He could probably find a cure for cancer as easily as he could help us militarily."

"I wholeheartedly agree," enthused his opposite number in MI5. "And this is a rare opportunity to show any aliens out there that Homo sapiens can be a force for good."

Agent Alpha adopted a more cynical tone. "We have no idea as to what his intentions are or even how many more of his kind are hiding in plain sight. And what happens when he reaches adulthood? I maintain that taking a blind leap of faith with this alien poses a huge risk to the safety of humankind."

"So, what do you suggest we do?" asked the field

marshal.

"I believe that we should terminate the creature's life," Agent Alpha said plainly. "Who knows what it's capable of once the anaesthetic wears off."

"With a heavy heart, I'm inclined to agree," the field marshal grimaced. "I propose we take a vote and act upon the majority decision immediately."

*

Later that night a neighbour of the Mortons was woken from his sleep by the constant thrum of a car engine. Padding outside in a dressing gown, he shone a torch on his neighbour's garage door and saw smoke billowing from its extremities. He phoned the police, who found the Morton family dead inside their carbon-monoxide-filled Volkswagen.

Is There a Doctor on Board?

"Please don't tell me that you're still working on that anthology of yours, Clive," Margo protested from the doorway to my study. "We should be on our way to the airport and you have yet to put the suitcases in the car."

My wife had clearly forgotten that I, Clive Bogarde, was England's pre-eminent writer and that my latest book was of far more importance to me than our yearly pilgrimage to the Grand Hotel Imperiale in Italy. And in any case I was already set for departure, resplendent in my trusty navy blazer, Panama hat and a Marylebone Cricket Club members' tie. "My dear, I am driven by some demon whom I can neither resist nor understand," I replied, paraphrasing Orwell.

"I wish that same demon would drive me to the airport," Margo huffed. "You can get off that computer right now and forget about writing for the next two weeks. You are completely obsessed."

As if that wasn't enough, the apple of my eye marched directly into my office and unplugged the computer from the mains. "Cripes!" I yelped as the screen went black.

By the resolute look on Margo's face, I arrived at the conclusion that the lady was not for turning. "Get your fat backside out of that chair and get down those stairs," she said acidly.

"But I've thought of a whizz idea for a new short story," I started to explain but my words fell on deaf ears as she bustled towards the stairs like a tweed tornado.

Loading the suitcases into the back of the Land Rover was a beastly struggle. Poor Margo was of little use on account of her osteoporosis and, at seventy-two years of age, I was also unsuited to physical exertion. Mind you, I once boxed for Oxford University and was very much the athlete in my youth. Between us we wrestled our luggage on board and were soon heading for Heathrow Airport.

Usually Margo was the designated driver but today, for some reason, I was at the helm. "Clive, why aren't you using the SatNav?" she enquired.

Frankly, I was aghast that she would even ask such a thing. "Because we've driven to Heathrow umpteen times, darling," I reminded her. "And the last thing I need is some dulcet-toned popsy calling out instructions for three hours solid."

Margo slipped a boiled sweet into her mouth and rested another on my knee. "I shan't be in the least bit surprised if you get lost," she declared.

Though I was concentrating on the road ahead, I could envisage the look of certainty on her face. "Nonsense!" I countered. "I know these roads as well as I know the back of my hands." As I said this, I actually studied the back of my hands in case I was asked to describe them.

Just then Margo sat bolt upright in her seat and waved her arms like an evangelist. "The iron! Did I unplug the iron before I left?" she yelped.

"Well, you unplugged my computer. That much I do know," I chuckled.

I took my eye off the road for a second. There was genuine alarm in her eyes. "You don't suppose I left it on, do you?" she asked, before typing on her phone for some unknown reason.

"How the devil would I know?" I replied. "I was minding my own business, writing my latest masterpiece. And anyway, it's too late to turn back now."

I glanced over and saw that Margo had regained her composure. "I've just texted Geoffrey. He has the spare key, remember?"

Our neighbour, Geoffrey, was entrusted to water houseplants and feed our cat in our absence despite him being a nosy little bastard.

"It wouldn't surprise me if he skulked into our house the moment we disappeared up the road," I grinned. "Probably looking through our filing cabinets or sifting through your underwear drawer as we speak—"

"Oh, don't be so critical, Clive," Margo snapped, staring at her phone screen. "Geoffrey is a pillar of the local community and, what's more, he loves cats."

"So did Blofeld," I quipped, pleased with my quick wit.

"Ah, he's texted back," said Margo, ignoring me. "And he's going straight over."

"I bet he is," I smirked.

*

I took a wrong turn ten miles from Heathrow and found myself driving through a quaint chocolate-box village replete with thatched-roofed cottages and a plethora of hanging baskets. "What a delightful hamlet," I said admiringly.

"You're lost, aren't you?" Margo snapped.

This was not a time to show weakness so I continued to gloss over the fact that I didn't know where we were. "What better sensory experience could there be than listening to Tchaikovsky whilst driving through the beautiful English countryside?" I enthused.

In my peripheral vision I could see that Margo had folded her arms. "I just knew you'd get lost," she said in a told-you-so voice.

I remained resolute. It was obvious that I was hopelessly lost – of course I was – but I'd be damned if I was going to admit it to her.

"I'll switch the SatNav on," Margo sighed. "Lest we end up in Wales."

"If you must."

*

Despite our scenic detour, we checked in with plenty of time to spare and subsequently cleared security. The absolute best thing about airports is the opportunity it affords me to people watch. Although it was still morning, several travellers could be seen tucking into caviar and quaffing Champagne at a franchise oyster bar.

"Who on earth would want to drink Champagne and eat oysters at eleven o'clock in the morning?" questioned Margo.

I stopped to regard them. A brood of showy types perched on high stools and with oyster juice dribbling down their chins. "The type of person who likes to be seen doing something ostentatious in a public place, one would assume."

Later, as I queued up to pay for toiletries in Boots the chemist, a man, whom I had earlier seen guzzling seafood at the oyster bar thought to push in front of me. Naturally I shoulder barged him out of the way and told him to get to the back of the line.

"But I have less items than you," he implored, as if that were a justifiable reason to jump a queue.

"Fewer," I corrected. "You have fewer items than me." It was clear to me that he had attended the wrong sort of school.

"But I have a plane to catch," he bleated.

"Well, we all have planes to catch," I replied. "It is, after all, the primary function of an airport, is it not?"

The chap let out a pathetic little whine and I caught a frightful whiff of his fishy breath. God, I would have loved to punch him in his dismal face. However, to give him his due, this halfwit wasn't one to give in easily. "You have a basketful of toiletries," he continued, "whereas I only have a stick of deodorant."

"Then why not double your items by finding yourself some minty mouthwash?" I suggested.

The twerp glared at me, deodorant in hand, but I stood my ground. "Had you asked me courteously, I would have gladly let you in," I said. "As it is, you have the manners of an ape and the breath of an otter. So keep quiet and wait in line, there's a good chap."

*

The flight to Milan took off on time and, as ever, the business-class menu was most agreeable. I tucked into an entrée of Tuscan veal rolls with porcini mushrooms washed down by a full-bodied Chianti. Margo opted for monkfish in a caper-and-olive sauce.

I was delighted to spot a copy of my best-selling novel *The De Montfort Murders* in the hands of a young female passenger and felt almost compelled to wander over and introduce myself. Not one to miss an opportunity to bolster my self-worth, I discreetly drew Margo's attention to the lady in question.

"The poor girl doesn't appear to be enjoying it," she teased. "Not everyone is a fan of your work, my dear. Let us not forget that critic with whom you locked horns on the *Talking Books* TV show."

I knew by my wife's catlike smile that she was deliberately pushing my buttons yet, like a fool, I still took the bait. "Percy Baskerville? That pompous old hack! He wouldn't know a split infinitive from a split pair of trousers!"

Just then a commotion a few rows ahead stole everyone's attention. Food trays were sent flying as a passenger erupted from his seat, clutching his throat and honking like a seal. A female cabin crew member rushed off in a blind panic to fetch help and the man's wife vigorously clouted his back as he hunched forward with his jowls flapping.

"Poor chap's choking on something, Margo," I grimaced, placing my food tray to one side and unbuckling my seatbelt.

With a scramble that belied my years, I was upon the unfortunate fellow in a flash and bear-hugging him into the aisle. I performed the Heimlich manoeuvre by thrusting my interlocked hands into his abdomen several times, hoping to dislodge whatever was wedged in his airways.

A desperate announcement came over the Tannoy, asking if there was a doctor on board. My charge was becoming limp in my arms and his wife frantically beseeched me to help him. I lay him on his back so I could dig my fingers into his mouth and down his throat. His eyes, meanwhile, had begun to roll back in their sockets and his face was turning a pale shade of blue.

Behind me, the privacy curtains between business and economy swished open dramatically and a man rushed in shouting that he was a doctor.

To my dismay, this medic was none other than the oyster-breathed queue jumper but, seeing that a man's life was hanging in the balance, I was greatly relieved to hand over to a professional, no matter who.

"I assume he has a piece of meat lodged in his throat," I explained, "but I can't reach it."

"The Heimlich manoeuvre will soon dislodge that," the doctor said with a certainty that bordered on arrogance.

"I've already tried that," I replied, worried that the man's life was ebbing away with every wasted second.

The physician hauled the unconscious man to his feet. "You obviously didn't do it properly," he sneered. "Heuuup!" he grunted, violently jerking the dying man in his dynamic embrace. "Heuuup!" he tried again.

"No-ooo! Please God, no!" wailed the man's wife as her husband flopped in the doctor's arms like a big rag doll.

Through force of effort, the doctor's face had turned puce and veins were bulging in his temples. "Heuuup!"

"This man needs an emergency tracheotomy," I stated. "Otherwise he will die within the next minute-or-so."

"A tracheotomy?" the doctor puffed, allowing the man to drop lifelessly to the floor. "I'm a doctor not a surgeon! I've done all I can for him."

"Right, get out of my way, you imbecile!" I thundered, springing into action. I'd seen a dramatic reconstruction of an improvised tracheotomy on television and knew exactly what to do. "Something sharp!" I yelled to the crew. "I need something sharp! Scissors, Swiss army knife, anything!"

I knelt over the victim and pulled a ballpoint pen from my blazer, removing its ink refill with my teeth.

A female attendant hurtled through and handed me a pair of nail scissors, prompting a chorus of fearful gasps from everyone in attendance.

The doctor stretched out a palm. "I strongly advise you not to attempt this," he sputtered.

"Get out of my eye line, you gutless pillock," I growled, feeling for the stricken man's Adam's apple and pressing the point of a scissor blade just below it. Under my breath, I prayed to God that my gamble would pay off then pressed down, piercing the cartilage and driving the blade into the dying man's trachea. Horrified screams rang out all around me but I stuck grimly to the task and wiggled the scissors to widen the incision. With a great deal of pressure I forced the ballpoint's plastic tube into the slit, whereupon there was a wondrous hiss as trapped air was released.

"Omigod, he's done it!" someone shouted as the man's eyelashes fluttered and his chest heaved.

His wife threw herself upon me as he began to regain consciousness. "You've saved his life," she sobbed. "You've saved his life."

It wasn't long before the man was sitting up and breathing like Darth Vader through the tube that was now protruding from his neck. Passengers swarmed to congratulate me on the miracle I had performed and dear Margo gazed at me with fresh adoration in her eyes. However, much as I enjoyed being fêted as a hero, all I could think about was how I could use this dramatic story in my book.

Brian the Bigot

Despite residing in Britain's friendliest hamlet, Britain's unfriendliest man, Brian Scragg, thought it a living hell. In fact the village of Goodchurch's prevailing ambience was so wholesomely happy that it caused his blood to boil and his teeth to itch. So unstoppably buoyant were its inhabitants that he could have cheerfully strangled every last one of them as they slept in their beds.

Scragg, a man who had no use for manners or deodorant, was the proprietor of Goodchurch's only newsagent's. Consequently, no matter how curmudgeonly or how offensively he behaved towards his customers, they made every allowance for him and continued on their merry way.

Brian's intolerance was as indiscriminate as it was exhaustive and very little escaped the scope of his enmity. His shop had become a bastion of bitterness and all who entered did so at their peril. As a child, he had delighted in pulling the legs off insects and smearing dog shit on doorknobs; as an adult, his aim was to make everyone else's lives as unpleasant as his own.

Having fetched the newspaper bundles in from the back of the shop and signed for a delivery of pre-packed sandwiches, he looked at his watch and released a joyless sigh. The time read 6.30, auguring the arrival of Mrs Clapham who, at this moment, would be putting in teeth and zipping up fur-trimmed ankle boots in readiness for her daily expedition to his store. As if caught in a time loop, Brian endured her popping in each day for the *Daily Express,* a bar of Cadbury's chocolate and some pointless chit-chat. He secretly wished she would die on her doorstep so he wouldn't have to spend another minute in her withering company. Soon she would arrive and start passing comment on the weather – as if he could care two hoots, seeing as he was stuck inside his wretched shop for seven days a week.

Sure enough, right on time, the door opened with a cheery ding-a-ling and in shuffled Mrs Clapham, nylon-wigged and as tall as a Hobbit. "Good day to you, Mr Scragg," she faltered, her thick makeup creviced by wrinkles. "Aren't we lucky to have such wonderful weather?"

"Oh, yes. Ever so lucky. I must remember to run up a flag in celebration."

Mrs Clapham responded by smiling impishly and wagging an arthritic finger. "You are such a jester, Mr Scragg. I never know if you're serious or not."

"Oh, I'm serious, you old bag."

"What was that?"

"I asked if you'd like a bag, Mrs Clapham."

"Oh, yes please. You are so very kind."

With her goods paid for, the pensioner turned unsteadily on her heels and shambled to the door while Brian looked on with contempt. His discourtesy towards Mrs Clapham was all the more spiteful considering he knew that the poor woman was dying from pancreatic cancer. He took pleasure in seeing her battle with the heavy door and, as she squeezed through, a little of the village's happiness edged into Scragg's shop like an unwelcome guest.

Next to offend Brian with their good looks and cheery disposition were married couple, Sanjay and Nathan, who popped in for a packet of cigarettes and a copy of *The Observer*. "And how are we today, Mr Scragg?" Sanjay enquired, using the first-person plural in a way that irritated the shopkeeper intensely.

"*We* would be fine if you learned to speak plain English, pal."

"Oh, look who's got out of the wrong side of bed this morning," Nathan chuckled.

"As per usual," added Sanjay with a roguish grin.

Homophobia and racism came as natural to Scragg as swimming does to a fish so this couple were his bitterest pill. "Look, unless you freaks are going to buy anything else, I suggest you piss off out of my shop."

"And there was us about to invite you over for dinner," Nathan teased.

The bigot's expression was one of pure loathing. "No offence, but I would rather pour vinegar in my eyes than socialise with a couple of queers."

"We do understand," smiled Sanjay, linking arms with

his husband in an act of defiance.

"You two sicken me!" Scragg called out as they drifted from the shop in a stream of smiles.

*

By late afternoon, Brian Scragg considered his day to have passed almost agreeably. He'd made a young boy cry, short-changed two pensioners to the tune of £20 and drawn some satisfaction from insulting everyone else who passed through.

What he didn't anticipate, though, was the entire village descending on his shop before closing time and gathering outside as if it had suddenly become a holy shrine. Their ranks swelled silently and doggedly, forming an unnerving barricade of resolute smiles and hawkish eyes. Even more of a surprise to Scragg was that Mrs Clapham, chaperoned by Nathan and Sanjay, doddered into the shop with a sawn-off shotgun clasped in her reedy hands.

"What the shitting hell is going on?" the shopkeeper asked, as hundreds of eyes peered through his grimy windows.

Sanjay was the first to speak. "Mrs Clapham called for a spur-of-the-moment meeting in the village hall this afternoon. As you can see, Mr Scragg, it was quite the turnout. The entire village, in fact."

"Get to the point, gay boy," sneered Brian, folding his arms.

A thin smile grew across Sanjay's face. "The point is

this, Mr Scragg. We are unanimously of the opinion that your incivility is starkly at odds with the convivial ethos of our village—"

"So? See if I care. You can all go to hell as far as I'm concerned."

"Interesting that you should mention going to hell," Sanjay continued. "I shall let Mrs Clapham take it from here."

The pensioner stepped forward and aimed the shotgun at Scragg's chest. The eyes of the village stared in silent fascination and their smiles grew wider. "You might think me an uncoordinated old fool, Mr Scragg, but I am certain that I shan't miss you from this range."

Scragg stared into both barrels of the gun. His mouth was suddenly dry, his words like sawdust. "Put that down, you scabby old cow. I doubt it's even loaded."

"Oh, it's loaded," the old lady purred, inching forward.

"You stupid woman, you can't possibly get away with shooting me. Besides, there's the CCTV—"

"The CCTV has already been taken care of," said Mrs Clapham. "Besides, who says that I want to get away with it? I'm slowly dying, not that you ever cared. The idea of spending my last few months being looked after in one of Her Majesty's prisons seems perfectly agreeable."

The villagers could taste the shopkeeper's fear and relished it. As one, they held their breath.

In a last-ditch attempt to save his life, Scragg attempted to rush the old lady, but not before she had giggled with delight and squeezed the trigger. With the villagers' applause ringing in her ears, Mrs Clapham looked down at her victim's bloodied body. "Goodbye, Mr Scragg. You will not be missed."

Fiona's Birthday

Galumphing into the garden, Fiona Bagshaw generated a damp, stormy blur of blonde hair and bingo wings. She stomped onto the patio, wrapped in a large bath towel and perfumed by shower gel, causing dahlia petals to scatter like pigeons.

"Where the bloody hell is he?" she muttered to herself before noticing that the shed door was wide open. The singular object of her pursuit, husband Donald, had last been seen in the living room surfing satellite TV channels dressed in a tiger-print onesie.

"What *on earth* are you doing?" she thundered, finding Donald glumly inspecting a paintbrush whose bristles had solidified into plastic.

"My brush has gone hard," he announced.

"Listen, if that's some kind of childish euphemism I'm really not interested."

"I was hoping to paint the garage door this weekend—"

"Well, can't this wait? May I remind you that it *is* my birthday and that we're supposed to be at Adriano's within the hour?"

"Hey, relax! I'm always dressed and ready before you anyway," he smirked. "Oooh, has someone forgotten to take their little HRT tablets?"

So Fiona, on her forty-ninth birthday, bellowed like a savage and sent him crashing into a stack of buckets with one violent shove of the garden rake. "And just so you know, James and Hayley have already arrived with the kids, so stop pratting about!"

"Babe, can you help me up?" he implored, showcasing puppy-dog eyes and a large plant pot that helmeted his head.

"You can piss off."

"Sorry about that," Fiona said in a sing-song voice, apologising to her daughter and son-in-law and their two children who had watched events unfold from the safe harbour of the conservatory. "Ooh, presents! Are they for me?"

*

After blow-drying her hair and squeezing into her favourite party dress, the one she'd bought specially to see Take That at Wembley, Fiona studied herself in the full-length mirror. *Only a small amount of podge and barely a wrinkle – not bad for forty-nine*, she thought while smoothing the contours of the dress.

Once downstairs, she was pleased to see that Donald had changed out of his onesie and was chatting with the others in the kitchen. Steadying herself against the tumble drier, she teetered on each leg in turn to slip on a pair of heels. From this low vantage point she glared at his Bart Simpson socks but noted that he looked sufficiently presentable otherwise.

"You smell nice," she said, sniffing Donald's neck with a cold suspicion that he might not have washed and deodorised himself. She deliberately neglected to mention that a large cobweb was conspicuously draped across his hair like a tatty doily. And judging by the duplicitous smirks on her daughter and son-in-law's faces, she wasn't the only one keeping this anomaly quiet.

Good, serves him bloody right, she thought, kissing her husband squarely on the lips and thanking him for being ready.

"Zip me up at the back, would you?" she asked Donald, pointing over her shoulder as if he might need reminding where her back was.

"Gordon Banks is the best goalkeeper in the world!" five-year-old Connor announced on his return from the bathroom.

"Gordon Banks?" Donald whooped. "Maybe forty-odd years ago! Where on earth did you pluck that name from?"

"From the man in the ceiling."

"What man in what ceiling?" Donald asked, squatting on his haunches to smile directly into his grandson's face.

"The man upstairs ... he said that England are playing West Germany in the World Cup Final tomorrow."

"You are hilarious," Donald chuckled before picking up Connor for a Superman ride. "Gordon Banks, eh? The name takes me right back to my own childhood...

Right, who's ready for pasta and pizza? C'mon birthday girl, let's go."

*

29th July, 2015, precisely one year later

Because today was her fiftieth birthday, and in the absence of an offer to join George Clooney aboard his yacht on Lake Como, Fiona took the afternoon off as annual leave from her job as project manager at Hammersmith and Fulham Council. Donald had enigmatically assured her that there would be a 'surprise' waiting for her on her return.

One thing was certain: whatever the surprise, it wasn't likely to bestow Fiona bragging rights over Monica Sutton and Tina Hollins. Monica had told everyone and anyone about her swanky fiftieth birthday at some lofty restaurant in The Shard; Tina, not to be outdone, crowed interminably about the fancy dinner her husband had arranged for her at Le Manoir aux Quat'Saisons.

"Raymond Blanc himself spoke to us in the herb garden, nuh, nuh, nuh," Fiona wittered to herself, impersonating Tina's supercilious tone while waiting for the traffic lights to change. She pondered the inevitable pallidity of her own impending celebration, her knuckles white as she squeezed the steering wheel. With his customary lack of ingenuity, Donald had booked a table at Adriano's.

"Babe, but you love it there," he had chirped after she'd

suggested a break from the norm. "Leave it to me, my sweet. I'll book your favourite table for eight o'clock."

After unlocking the front door and flinging her keys onto the hallway dresser, Fiona immediately became aware that the sum total of his 'surprise' was a large card and a bottle of Tesco Prosecco, festooned with a pink bow. Just then, she was alarmed by a series of loud metallic noises emanating from upstairs when, to the best of her knowledge, she should have been the only person in the house.

The birthday girl tentatively placed one foot on the bottom stair and craned her neck to listen to the continuing commotion. "Donald! Is that you making all that racket?" She instinctively grabbed the wooden giraffe figurine they had brought home from Kenya and held it like a baseball bat before venturing further.

When she reached the landing, the hatch to the loft was fully open and a large spanner lay directly beneath it. Furthermore, the metallic clangour therein was accompanied by some exuberant whistling from a person yet unseen. Perplexed, Fiona couldn't understand why Donald hadn't warned her about work being carried out in the house. She also wondered why there wasn't a tradesman's van in the driveway.

She shouted up, crowding her hands around her mouth in the manner of an Alpine yodeller. "Hello! Hello-o! It's Mrs Bagshawww! Whoever's up there, can you hear me?"

The clanging stopped and a young male voice rang out from the darkness. "Oh hello, madam. You must be the lady of the house."

"Yes, I am. What exactly are you doing up there?" she enquired, hoping to see the man behind the voice. "Clearly my prat of a husband has forgotten to warn me."

"I'm plumbing in a new water tank," he answered, his face partly shadowed.

The workman didn't appear to be carrying a torch and Fiona wondered why he would choose to work in the dark. "Oh? So what was wrong with the old one?"

"Uh, don't rightly know, madam." The voice was hesitant. "Now you've got me."

Fiona envisaged him scratching his head. "Did my husband get in contact with you? Was he here earlier?"

"Um, I'm fairly certain he left me a key—"

"Fairly certain?" Fiona huffed. "Have you developed some form of amnesia, young man?"

Increasingly concerned at the vagueness of this whole improbable turn of events, Fiona stared up at the rafters, hands on hips, hoping for some answers. Crouching over the opening, the young man's features appeared in full light. She noticed that the fellow was fresh-faced and handsome. As he leaned forward, an errant tendril of hair tumbled from his otherwise slick coiffure.

He got on his knees and extended one arm through the open hatch. "Could you please do me a favour, madam? Throw me that spanner up, would you?"

"Yeah, yeah, sure," she answered, bending to grasp the tool before hurling it towards his outstretched fingers.

"Cor, great throw missus!" he chuckled, waving it as

if it were a flag.

From what she could see of him, Fiona guessed the plumber to be barely into his twenties. For such a young lad, he had an old-fashioned way about him, which she found endearing.

"Could I offer you a tea, coffee, soft drink?" she asked, watching the heels of his work boots disappear from view.

"Ooh, lovely," he chirped, his broad smile reappearing from the shadows. "Tea, please. White, two sugars."

While waiting for the kettle to boil, Fiona called Donald's mobile hoping for some clarification but it went straight to voicemail. Returning to the landing, she took a chair from the guest bedroom and stood on it while lifting the mug of tea. *Why on earth has he returned the loft ladder to its stowed position?* she wondered. *Must be one of those daft health and safety rules they have to adhere to.*

"Tea's ready!" she yelled, still baffled as to why the young man hadn't turned on the fluorescent light.

"Oh, thank you so much. Just the ticket," he said, liberating the mug from her grasp with a pincer movement. Fiona was struck by the familiarity of his face; she felt certain she had seen him before somewhere.

"Is your old man looking forward to the big game tomorrow?" he breezed. "I've managed to bag a ticket and I'm just so excited."

"Oh, what game is that?" Fiona asked.

"England against West Germany. World Cup Final! What game, indeed."

"Ha, ha, very funny ... although I'm female I *do* know that the last time England was in a World Cup Final was the year they won it in 1966. And I should know – my father died on the way to the game, hit by an ambulance."

Hesitancy crept into the young man's voice. "Please forgive me, madam... I don't want to disrespect the memory of your father but how could he have been run over by an ambulance on the way to a match that hasn't happened yet?"

Exasperated by his game-playing nonsense, Fiona stepped down from the chair with a shake of her head. Though initially likeable, the boy's vagueness and his weird sense of humour had become irksome.

"OK, I'll leave you to carry on!" she shouted brusquely.

Then, just as she was about to try Donald's number for the second time, the young man called down to her. "Thanks for the tea, madam. I'd better crack on as I need to get home early – it's my daughter's first birthday today."

"Oh? It's my birthday today as well!" she countered, her interest rekindled. "What is your daughter's name?"

"Fiona," he replied, disappearing from view.

Fiona was immediately thrown by the stark curiousness of his remark. "What...? Wait! *What* did you just say?" She repositioned the chair under the hatch. "Hey! Hey!! What did you say?" Her voice was urgent now as she suddenly remembered where she'd seen his face before: the black-and-white framed photograph on her mother's mantelpiece.

Kicking the chair to one side, she snatched a hooked pole from the airing cupboard and scrambled the loft ladder down onto the carpet. Frantically she clambered up the rungs but, when she pulled the switch cord, her father was gone.

The Fable of the Fisherman's Hat

Outopia – a fishing village in Ancient Greece 328 BC

Demetrius the fisherman woke before the rooster's first crow while the inky Aegean Sea was still slumbering in its abyss. From their bed his wife, Isadora, heard him muddle his way around in the dark, blindly feasting on a breakfast of stale bread and fish washed down with a goblet of wine.

Isadora, whose kindness was more pronounced than her beauty, lit a lamp that illuminated both her plain-looking face and the swell of her breasts. "Return to our bed and make me feel like a woman, sweet Demetrius," she purred.

And so, because his wife was his moon and stars, Demetrius slipped under the covers and made love to her until she could barely remember her own name.

Soon the sea was awake just fifty paces from their door, rattling the pebbled beach with its first sluggish waves. Birds welcomed the dawn by chirruping from the house's reed-thatched roof and the cockerel cleared its throat with a raucous yodel.

After gifting Isadora a parting kiss, Demetrius, wearing no more than a loincloth and robe, tramped barefoot towards his boat. While his beloved wife could best be described as homely, he was a handsome man in the prime of his life with hair black as squid ink and a body knotted with muscles. With joy in his soul, he closed his eyes and opened his nostrils, inhaling the briny air as the ascending sun caused steam to rise from damp fishing nets.

His fragile sailboat was a rustic affair fashioned from papyrus and with barely enough space to accommodate even a modest haul of fish. A sophisticated Athenian might have scoffed at such a simple life but Demetrius was abundantly happy with his carefree existence and his adoring wife.

From a long wooden box that he kept inside the boat the young fisherman produced his lucky yellow hat, the one that made him the envy of every man in Outopía. Whence the hat came he had no idea; he had found it washed up on the beach one morning, as if the gods had gifted it to him for some unspecified reason. Yellow as an egg yolk, the hat was cone-shaped and of a style he had never seen before – a style he knew straightaway would set him apart from all of the other fishermen.

On the day he'd discovered it, Demetrius had wasted no time in donning his godsend and found it to be a perfect fit. He had gazed at his reflection in a pail of water and was especially pleased with what he saw. The cone was as long as his arm and rose like a sunlit stalagmite from his head.

He had swaggered about the village that day, his towering hat attracting the admiration of all who were fortunate enough to witness it. Without exception, the villagers were an unsophisticated bunch and very easily pleased, which explains why the men were struck with envy and the women with feverish desire. And when the spectacular headpiece had first caught Isadora's eye, she couldn't help but fall headlong in love with the man wearing it, making Demetrius the happiest fisherman in Outopía from that day hence.

With help from two other fishermen, Demetrius slid his craft down the stony beach until it glided into the shallows. He waded merrily alongside until it began to float then clambered aboard, causing the boat to rock from side to side until it found its balance. He saluted the men with a cheery wave, leaving them to hanker after his amazing hat as he rowed out to sea.

"Is there a happier man in the whole of Greece?" said one fishermen to the other.

"Demetrius has every reason to be happy," his friend replied. "He has his own boat, an affectionate wife and a hat that I would give my right arm for. What more could a fellow need?"

"That hat alone would make my life complete," confessed the first fisherman.

*

Once in deeper waters, Demetrius trusted his vessel to the wind and opened its sail. When he found a suitable fishing spot he dropped anchor and cast his net, prompting a pod of dolphins to appear as they knew that humans customarily shared their catch.

The untroubled sky spread out in every direction and the jubilant fisherman was at one with nature. "What better life could there be?" he shouted into the wind.

In due course the net became heavy, so heavy that Demetrius struggled to haul it in. The dolphins carved circles in the water, excited at the prospect of a free meal. It took all of the young man's strength to heave the bulging net from the sea and it landed with an almighty thud, causing the boat to rock wildly and take in seawater. Demetrius frantically bailed out the incoming water but the weight of the catch forced the rim of his flimsy craft to sit level with the surface of the sea. At the same time the wind picked up and the waves became lively, exacerbating his problem.

Although it pained him to do so, he had no option but to shovel bucketloads of anchovies and sprats back into the sea, sending the dolphins into a feeding frenzy. Still the sea slopped in, putting his vessel in immediate danger of capsizing.

Just as he had halved his load, Demetrius's bucket hit something solid. The beleaguered fisherman, now up to his waist in seawater, could barely believe his eyes. A white-limbed *thing* was struggling to free itself from the silvery heap of thrashing fish. Though he was sinking fast, Demetrius dug his hands in and extracted a well-upholstered baby boy who smiled in his arms and kicked his pudgy legs in every conceivable direction.

Despite the hull of the boat disappearing below the surface with him still standing in it, in a typical moment of blind optimism Demetrius saw the infant as another gift from the gods. "Sweet child, I take you as my son," he pledged, holding the boy aloft. "Hereafter you shall be known as Plutus, son of Demetrius."

"I strongly doubt that," the baby replied, causing the fisherman's eyes to bulge from their sockets as he began to tread water. "You see, I am Theseus, son of Poseidon."

"Poseidon?" Demetrius gargled, holding the silver-tongued boy with outstretched arms and swallowing seawater as he spoke. "If you are truly the son of Poseidon, why has he abandoned you?"

"He would never abandon me," said the baby haughtily. "He left me alone on a nearby island so that I might learn to be independent. If I were to meet with danger, I only had to blow into a magic conch shell and he would rush to rescue me."

Demetrius's arms were becoming tired so he floated the baby on the water while the dolphins continued to fill their bellies. "Then why didn't you blow into this magical shell of yours the moment you became adrift in this treacherous sea?"

"Because the shell is still on the island, you fool. I was dragged from the shoreline by a strong current before I had a chance to react."

While Demetrius was still struggling to come to terms with the fact that he was conducting an adult conversation with a baby – and that he was in danger of drowning – one of the dolphins chimed in. "As you have been kind to us, human, we could take you to the island. It's not that far."

"You can speak?" spluttered the fisherman.

"Of course I can speak! Why you should find a talking dolphin any more astonishing than a talking baby is beyond me."

"I meant no offence," said Demetrius, trying to keep his head and hat above water.

"None taken," replied the dolphin. "Climb on my back, human. The infant can do likewise."

The fisherman and the baby rode on the glossy back of the lead dolphin while the others undulated in and out of the waves as they sped alongside.

"This is such fun!" shouted Demetrius as the salty spray spattered his tanned face.

"You are so easily pleased," said Theseus as he clung to the fisherman's waist.

The island soon came into view, fronted by a white sandy beach set against a backdrop of cypress trees and olive groves. The lead dolphin offloaded its passengers into the shallows and bade them good luck before swimming away. Demetrius, grateful to have lost neither life nor hat, waded to the shore with the heavy baby in his arms.

Upon reaching the beach, Theseus directed a podgy finger at the magic conch shell. "And there it is, fisherman! Exactly where I left it."

As the infant toddled across the sand to retrieve the horn the momentousness of what was about to happen unnerved Demetrius. "So with just one blow on that shell the mighty Poseidon will come to your aid, you say?"

"Of course," replied the baby. "And knowing my father, he will want to reward you for your heroic rescue."

"Oh, I don't want any fuss. If your father could simply get me back to Outopía, I would be delighted. All that I could possibly need is there."

Theseus was bemused by the man's humility. "Listen carefully to my words, humble fisherman. Surely you have need of a new boat? How else will you earn a livelihood? How else will you feed yourself?"

Demetrius listened keenly. "Are you saying that your father could build me a new boat?"

"He built the great walls of Troy so a small boat is hardly likely to tax him."

Without further ado, Theseus blew mightily into the conch shell, the sound reminiscent of a wolf's lonely howl on a windless night. The siren pealed through olive groves and reverberated across the sea, causing birds to take flight and shoals of fish to change course.

A breathless calm ensued. Visoring their eyes against the sun, the peculiar twosome stared out towards the horizon where a speck of something dynamic advanced at high speed.

"My father," confirmed Theseus, with a self-satisfied look on his cherubic face.

As the speck grew larger so did Demetrius's unease. Poseidon, even in the mid-distance, was as monumental as legend had suggested. He drove a large shell chariot pulled by four fish-tailed horses that galloped so fast their hooves barely skimmed the water's surface. Soon the Titan was close enough for Demetrius to study him in detail. Fringed by a curly beard, Poseidon's expression was one of stormy determination. His mighty hands held the reins of a golden bridle as the cloak that draped his muscular body billowed in the breeze.

With much churning of water, the chariot came to a halt a stone's throw from the beach. Poseidon glared at the fisherman with deep suspicion and dropped into the surf with his trident in his hand. "I am Poseidon, god of the sea and brother to Zeus and Hades," he boomed. "Who art thee, human?"

"I am Demetrius, husband of Isadora," the fisherman squeaked as the sea god waded towards him.

Theseus was the next to speak. "Father, I have much to thank this human for. I was lost at sea without the magic shell and he rescued me."

By this time Poseidon was looming over Demetrius, as large as a tree and near enough that the fisherman could feel the coldness of the sea emanating from his skin. Even including his tall hat, Demetrius stood no higher than the Titan's knees and he had to lean back to look up into his aquamarine eyes.

"A rarity," said Poseidon, placing an enormous hand on the fisherman's shoulder. "A mortal who hath proved himself to be of some use. I am in thy debt, noble fisherman. Ask something of me and it shall be done."

Demetrius was almost too afraid to ask but, given tacit encouragement by Theseus, took the plunge. "I am now without a fishing boat, your mightiness. And if it pleases you, the simplest of vessels would be more than enough."

"Ha! Is that all?" Poseidon chuckled, pointing his trident out to sea. "Behold thy new boat, human."

Following the direction indicated, the sight that befell Demetrius astonished him and brought him to the brink of tears. Anchored within swimming distance from the beach was a sturdy sailboat crafted from oak and coated in resin. His lips were all of a quiver. "F-for me? I don't know what to say. It's simply beautiful. I am indebted to you, my most generous master."

Poseidon, though not always well-disposed towards humans, had instantly warmed to this one. "Not only that, but I gift thee a key to my underwater palace. Knoweth that it is yours to visit anytime thee wish." He took from his seaweed belt a piece of coral that sparkled in the sun's rays and handed it to Demetrius.

The fisherman turned the coral in his hand, hoping that by doing so it might reveal its purpose. Poseidon smiled at the human's confusion and sought to explain. "Provided thou hast this piece of magic coral in thy grasp, thee can swim from anywhere in my watery realm and it will lead thee safely to my palace. Let it be thy lungs, human, as well as thy guide."

These were Poseidon's parting words. He scooped up his son in one huge hand and, without so much as a backward glance, waded out to his chariot and hurtled towards the horizon.

Demetrius watched the sea wash away the giant's footprints and pondered his next move. Should he sail home in his new boat or should he take a quick look at

Poseidon's underwater palace? He noted that the sun was still high in the sky and elected for the latter.

With his splendid hat fitted tightly to his head, and with the magic coral clasped firmly in his hand, Demetrius dived into an incoming wave. The magical power of the coral took over and soon he was being propelled through ever-deeper water, moving with ease and without needing to hold his breath. Several fathoms down, at a depth to which no human could possibly dive, his ears collected the mournful groans and sonar clicks of the ocean. Through the murky water he saw the subterranean palace impossibly lit by a million candles.

The fisherman walked on the sea bed, his yellow hat floating vertically above his head, completely overawed by the spectacle before him. A colonnade of coral columns marked the edifice's grand entrance and led him into an enormous building that existed in a gargantuan pocket of air.

As if in a dream, Demetrius stepped onto an expansive pearl floor ornamented with calcified starfish. Dotted around the superstructure were several life-size statues of the gods, Poseidon's being the most prominent. On the palace's periphery were verdant gardens replete with anemones and seagrasses. Bees fizzed from one pretty flower to the next and the trees were alive with birdsong. He could see candles everywhere, their flames dancing like fairies, swathing the palace in a golden radiance.

A sudden chorus of female voices, lilting and mellifluous, released Demetrius from his wonderment. He looked for their point of origin and, in a day already filled with surprises, beheld a trio of mermaids beckoning him from a rock pool by the canal's edge. Beguiled by their ethereal beauty, the fisherman quickened his pace and stood before them. Not one shared the same hair colour; all were white of skin and firm of breast.

"Good day, handsome mortal," greeted the raven-haired mermaid. "Come, free yourself from your wet clothes and join us in the pool."

"You can leave them to dry on the rocks," advised the flame-haired one.

"And we promise not to bite," chuckled the blonde.

Forgetting that he was presently married to the most wonderful woman in Outopía, the fisherman shed his simple clothes and jumped into the pool.

*

While in the grip of carnal desire Demetrius had lost all sense of time and place, not to mention his virtue. The mermaids had taken turns to pleasure him in ways he had never known existed and the numerous goblets of wine, served to him by a talking octopus, had caused him to lose all inhibitions.

During a period of rest, as the mermaids nibbled at his ears and stroked his hair, the fisherman gazed up at the glass-domed ceiling. Above it sat one thousand fathoms of seawater and Demetrius, despite his three beautiful distractions, began to wonder if it was still daylight. He stood up just as the blonde mermaid was ducking her head under the water for the third time. "As much as

I would love to stay, I must leave before sunset. If not, my voyage home will prove perilous."

"Oh, but you will return tomorrow, won't you?" pouted the redhead.

"You are the first mortal of whom we have had the pleasure," added the raven-haired mermaid before he had the chance to reply.

"And what a fine mortal you are," said the blonde.

"Of course I shall return tomorrow," Demetrius grinned while drying himself. "I have had the time of my life."

Seeing the human don his tall yellow hat jogged the flame-haired mermaid's memory. "Oh, human. We were inspired by your hat and wondered if you might accept this token of our appreciation."

As one, they emerged from the rock pool, stood up on their tails and presented Demetrius with a simple crown fashioned from sage leaves. "Let it be a reminder of our joyous day together," they said in unison.

Demetrius fastened his loincloth and flung his robe over one shoulder before trying on the wreath. "It fits perfectly," he enthused.

"And it makes you look even more handsome," flattered the redhead.

"Do you think so?" asked the fisherman, his ego suddenly as big as the ocean.

"Most assuredly!" they chorused.

The fisherman promptly bade farewell to the mermaids and thanked the octopus for his service. With the magic coral in his grasp, he headed for the surface feeling twice the man he had been previously.

Demetrius broke through the waves, relieved to see that the sun hadn't yet dipped its toes into the ocean and was hanging onto the darkening sky by its fingertips. Still excited by the day's adventures, he hauled himself onto his boat with the aid of a rope ladder and set sail for home.

As the crimson sky began to blacken, his new vessel cut through the sea at a dramatic rate of knots and the fisherman hollered his appreciation, hoping that Poseidon might hear him. Soon, though, he was as lonely as a clam under the canopy of night with only the moon and stars to guide him.

In due course, Outopía appeared in the distance, twinkling like a low-lying constellation. As his craft drew nearer, Demetrius was surprised to see a legion of villagers assembled on the shoreline. Isadora stood in their midst with a worried look on her face. Many held lanterns that lent a spectral glow to their weather-beaten faces. None at first recognised Demetrius because of the beautiful boat he was steering.

The errant fisherman dropped anchor in the moonlit water as a refrain of relieved cheers broke out from those assembled. "The gods have guaranteed his safe return!" shouted one villager.

"They have even given him a new boat!" yelled another.

Holding his old pointed hat above the sea's surface, Demetrius waded back to shore. He was relieved to be under the cover of darkness as he felt certain his guilt was evident for all to see.

Isadora was the first to greet him. "Oh, Demetrius, my sweet, sweet husband. When you didn't return by the afternoon, I feared greatly for your life."

"As did we all," added Spiros the carpenter.

"Well, I'm pleased to report that I am alive and well," Demetrius responded sheepishly. "And what a day I've had. To cut a long story short, I saved Poseidon's son from the sea and in return he has gifted me this boat."

"Wow!" the villagers marvelled collectively.

"Poseidon!" they gasped as one.

Plato, a villager who shared the great philosopher's name but sadly none of his intelligence, was next to speak. "Demetrius, my friend, why aren't you wearing your magnificent hat?"

Demetrius pointed to the simple wreath that encircled the circumference of his head. "I have a better hat now," he boasted.

"I think not," said Plato, wrinkling his nose. "As far as I can tell, that is just a ring of sage leaves."

"Who told you that this so-called hat is better than the other one?" frowned Prometheus the potter.

"Um, Poseidon himself," Demetrius lied.

"Well, I hate to disagree with a god," continued Plato, "but a tatty crown of leaves cannot possibly compete with your other hat."

"If it pleases you that much, you are welcome to keep my other hat," Demetrius sulked, handing it over.

Plato's eyes were suddenly as big as duck eggs. "As Zeus is my witness, I shall honour this noble hat!" he said excitedly, trying it on.

"It looks better on you than it did on Demetrius!" shouted Spiros.

"This is easily the best day of my life!" roared Plato as the villagers, in their excitement, forgot all about Demetrius and his shiny new boat. They raised the new custodian of the yellow hat aloft on their shoulders as if he were a conquering hero and carried him to the taverna for a night of drunken celebration.

The beach promptly cleared until only Demetrius and Isadora remained. "You have had quite the day, my love," she said, stroking his dark hair. "Let them have their fun, my brightest star. We have each other and that's all that matters."

For the first time since he had met her, Demetrius saw only plainness where he'd previously seen beauty in his wife's honest face. And he began to look upon her body with disdain, noticing that it wasn't as firm or as enticing as those of the mermaids with whom he had spent the afternoon. Under a bat-ridden sky, and with the sound of music and laughter emanating from the taverna, the couple returned to their marital home.

Once the sea was alone, it whispered its watery secrets and drifted into a deep sleep.

*

Having resorted to drinking heavily the previous night, Demetrius overslept and woke with a resounding head-ache. Daylight drifted into the shack and the sage crown lay in tatters across his pillow. He left the marital bed to down a flagon of water as Isadora called out to him, "Return to our bed, sweet Demetrius, and make me feel like a woman."

"Not today," he snapped, rejecting his wife for the first time since they were wed. "It's late and I need to take to the sea."

Isadora was deeply hurt and not a little taken aback but thought it best not to show her dejection out of consideration for her husband. "What are you looking for, my love?" she asked as he vigorously rummaged through the folds of his robes.

His voice was storm-tossed and frantic. "My piece of coral, woman! I had a piece of coral tucked into my loincloth!"

"Oh, that! I saw it last night while I was tidying up and threw it back into the sea. Such a fuss, my fine husband. It was only a piece of coral."

Demetrius was beside himself with anguish and ran out into the sunshine, wailing into his hands and cursing his bad fortune. Through doleful eyes he surveyed his simple domain and the vastness of the Aegean Sea. The universe didn't seem as perfect to him now as it had before. And to make matters worse, he could see his relinquished yellow hat glowing golden in the morning sun. It sat high and glorious on the head of Plato, the happiest man in Outopía.

The Leech

Its sound infiltrated a dream and then became a reality as Hiromi Osako woke to the harsh beep of his digital alarm at 6 a.m. He automatically sat upright on the futon, gathered his senses and fumbled for his spectacles. Then, with very little enthusiasm, he slid onto the tatami mat and adjusted the waistband of his pyjama shorts as he stood.

As was the case every morning, the first thing to invade his consciousness was a crystalline vision of his nemesis, Tatsuki Kitano, along with the snotty expression that never left the louse's conceited face. Although Hiromi Osako was a meek young man known for his passivity, he had once mused that he would likely think twice before throwing water on Kitano should the bastard ever catch fire.

After washing his face and shaving the few hairs that had bothered to grow on it, Hiromi regarded his features in the bathroom mirror. Firstly, there existed an unremarkable sweep of black hair that flopped across his head in a state of exhaustion; secondly, a soft-chinned, cherubic face, and thirdly, bespectacled eyes that carried in them all the sorrow of the world. Hiromi's lips, which were plump and feminine, rarely moulded themselves into a smile these days – not since Kitano had become his office supervisor and made his working life a living hell.

After breakfasting on packet noodles and a cup of oolong tea, Hiromi left his Tokyo apartment dressed in regulation black suit coupled with a subdued tie. He walked to the metro and stepped down into the bowels of the subway where a crow-black tide of similarly suited salarymen engulfed the station. Female office workers, obliged to follow the same dress code as the men, paired black pencil skirts and jackets with white button-down shirts. Most had tied silk scarves to their designer handbags to add a splash of colour.

Hiromi waited in line on the platform, a queue several people deep, and watched three trains come and go before it was his turn to board. As usual the carriage was as crammed as a bucketful of potatoes and those closest to the doors were shoved on board by the white-gloved attendants.

Once the doors were shut, Hiromi made an attempt to grab a ceiling strap but instead ended up with his face pushed up hard against the polycarbonate window with his spectacles askew. The train pulled away as the young man's lips began to spread across one side of his compressed face.

Upon reaching Shinjuku station, Hiromi checked his watch and followed the upward flow of the crowd, electing to take the stairs rather than allow the sluggish escalators to impede his progress.

His workplace was a project management office located on the eleventh floor in one of the district's many skyscrapers. As he rose in the elevator, the spectre of Kitano and his sneaky ways loomed large in his mind. Known for his diligence and humility, Hiromi was one of numerous unsung heroes responsible for the prosperity of the Japanese economy. In sharp contrast, Kitano was a man who had climbed the rungs of the corporate ladder on the backs of people like Hiromi. To create a good impression in front of his bosses, Kitano ensured he was the first to arrive and last to leave but, without them knowing, did very little in between.

Hiromi stepped tentatively into the office and bowed to all present. His nemesis lay in wait, dressed in a fake Armani suit and ready to cast his first insult of the day. "Osako-san," he smirked. "Please feel free to turn up whenever it suits you. I'd hate to think that our work here is getting in the way of your beauty sleep."

Hiromi regarded the office clock and saw that he had arrived a full thirty minutes before he was required to. Nevertheless, he chose not to fight his corner. "I seek forgiveness, supervisor Kitano, and promise to do better," he said, bowing obsequiously.

A smug look appeared on Kitano's bloodless face as he reloaded his mouth. "Osako-san, I am entrusting you with a trainee today. He's a postgrad and joins us on a one-year contract. I imagine he'll be another loser like you but I still expect you to do your best."

Hiromi nodded his head. "Understood, supervisor. I

look forward to meeting him."

"Ah, here he is now," said Kitano, clicking his fingers in the direction of a young man who had tiptoed into the office. "Endo-san! Over here!"

Scuttling forward, the newcomer bowed respectfully to all and sundry. Hiromi liked him instantly; he appeared to be a bashful, well-presented fellow, much like himself.

The supervisor initiated the introductions. "Endo-san, meet Osako-san who will be your induction trainer. Don't let Osako-san's dopey appearance fool you as he is actually highly intelligent, so listen and learn." Then, leaving the young men to become acquainted, Kitano addressed the room. "Listen up, everyone! Staff meeting in twenty minutes!"

"It is a great pleasure to meet you, Osako-san," said the trainee. "I will strive to do my best."

Hiromi warmed to the rookie and his polite demeanour. "May I ask your first name, Endo-san?"

"Ryuki," the young man replied with an enthusiastic nod. "And yours?"

"Hiromi."

There was an undeclared understanding between the two that they would never address each other by their first names again; nonetheless, it felt good to share a personal detail.

The recruit moved in closer, sensing he could breach etiquette without his instructor taking offence. "Osako-san, is supervisor Kitano always so rude to people?"

Hiromi smiled and kept his voice low. "Only to his subordinates. Anyone above his rank gets the five-star treatment." Then, feeling he was being disloyal to a co-worker in the presence of someone he had only just met, Hiromi buttoned his lip.

The new boy sensed his discomfort. "It's fine, Osako-san. You can dish the dirt and I won't think badly about you for doing so. I would prefer to know who I can trust rather than find out the hard way."

Hiromi, relieved to find someone he could open up to, neglected his usual propriety and spilled some of his beans. "My job is to develop strategies that help our business to become more effective but Kitano rips off my best ideas and takes all the credit."

"But that's reprehensible," said the newcomer, his kind eyes darkened by the ink of disapproval. "How can he be allowed to get away with it?"

"Because his superiors think he's wonderful and are taken in by him. I invariably work late to finish projects, only for him to leave my name off the presentations so he can pass them off as his own. It's so unfair. I pride myself on my work and strive to do my best for this company but sadly I see nothing for my endeavour." Seeing himself through another's eyes, Hiromi thought it best to stop as he didn't want to appear bitter and twisted.

"Could you not file a complaint?" the novice asked. "Surely someone would take your side."

Hiromi was taken aback by the newcomer's naivety. "It would be my word against his and he would always win. He has the bosses wrapped around his little finger and ensures that I'm not on their radar. To add insult to injury, the section manager is retiring this month and Kitano is certain to take his place, despite being wholly undeserving of the position… Anyway, enough about my inconsequential woes. We have a staff meeting to attend."

Hiromi provided Ryuki with the lyrics to the company song so that he could sing along with the others before the meeting started. The trainee saw at first-hand how Kitano turned on the charm in the presence of the outgoing section manager and brainstormed ideas as if they were his own. He also noticed how the supervisor talked over the women as if their views didn't matter.

"Listen, people! One more thing—" Kitano piped as the meeting drew to a close. "You are all aware that our CEO, Mr Suzuki, is paying us a visit from head office tomorrow so I want desks tidy and everyone on their best behaviour."

Returning to his desk, Hiromi impressed upon his apprentice the core values of the company and how important it was to work hard as a team. "Unity is strength, Endo-san. Regardless of who takes the praise, it's the welfare of the company that matters most."

The newcomer was amazed by his instructor's selflessness and thought it unfair that such a man could work so tirelessly and have nothing to show for his effort. "Can't the bosses further up the chain see the supervisor for what he is?" he asked with an innocence that Hiromi found endearing.

"I'm sure they would if they worked with him," replied Hiromi with a despondent sigh. "This is a family-run business, and the CEO is an inspirational guy who started with nothing. I'd love to spend some time with him tomorrow but the bosses keep him away from the workers each time he visits."

"Well, I find your restraint admirable," the trainee remarked. "I don't know how you remain so calm."

Hiromi leaned in as if about to divulge a very dark secret. "This is strictly between you and me, Endo-san, but in my head I call Kitano 'The Leech'."

"Most apt," smiled Ryuki, sensing that this was the only way that his mild-mannered trainer could secure some kind of moral victory.

Hiromi, feeling he was baring his soul more than was prudent, swivelled his chair to face the computer monitor and adopted a more serious tone. "Enough of this small talk, Endo-san. We have work to do."

*

At lunchtime Hiromi took his charge to an *udon* noodle restaurant that stood in a side street lined with bicycles and lanterns. The young men sat on high stools and leant against a service counter of blond wood, discussing topics ranging from *manga* to Japanese baseball. They never once intruded into each other's personal life; to do so would have been impolite. Hiromi found his understudy an intelligent, cultured fellow and hoped he would stay with the company for years to come.

As they walked together on the skyscraper-lined thoroughfare that led back to their office, Hiromi caught sight of Minato Yoshida, one of Japan's most famous movie stars. "Try not to stare, Endo-san," he squeaked from one side of his mouth, "but we are sharing the same sidewalk as Minato Yoshida!"

Almost as if he had heard his name mentioned, the middle-aged superstar appeared to deviate and walk straight towards them, his Burberry coat flapping in the breeze. Not only that, a broad smile lit up his illustrious face.

"Ryuki!" the luminary greeted. He offered a Western handshake, which Hiromi's associate met with a practised familiarity. Thereafter the two proceeded to chat like old friends, leaving Hiromi completely baffled as to what was going on. After introducing his starstruck colleague, it was Ryuki who brought an end to the conversation by saying that they had important work to do.

"Well, don't let me keep you. And please send my best regards to your mother and father," urged the movie star, charisma oozing from every pore.

"I'll be sure to," replied Ryuki, parting with a handshake and a mannerly bow.

Hiromi was momentarily rendered speechless and goggled at his new friend as if he had descended from Mars. "Omigod, how do you know Minato Yoshida?" he gasped.

"Oh, he's an old family friend," Ryuki said casually, as if it were no big deal.

Hiromi shook his head and led the way back to the office. "You are quite the surprise package, Endo-san."

*

On their return, The Leech was seen imposing his will on Yui Kishi, one of the female members of staff. Yui was a rebellious young lady whose black hair was dyed peroxide blonde and whose scowl was a permanent fixture. Kitano had ordered her to make his client a coffee, having already given her the menial task of photocopying a pile of documents even though he knew she had more important things to do.

Yui was not happy and her scowl had become even more pronounced. "How is it you only ever ask the girls to fetch coffee, supervisor Kitano?" she protested.

"Because it's what you women do best, Kishi-san," he hissed. "Besides, if you found yourself a husband, you wouldn't have to work here, now would you? Coffee – white, one sugar, little girl. And don't keep my client waiting."

Hiromi and Ryuki imagined the young woman's glare burning holes into the supervisor's jacket as he swaggered back to his private office. As soon as he was out of earshot, Yui called him a sexist pig.

*

By the time Hiromi and his apprentice's working day was over, night had descended on Tokyo and the city had begun to pulse. An amalgam of neon signs, loud J-pop music and giant digital screens heightened their senses as they walked to Shinjuku rail station, taking shortcuts past clamorous *pachinko* parlors, *izakaya* pubs and *yakitori* restaurants. The karaoke bars were already filling up with the *nomikai* crowds of office workers letting off steam after a hard day's work.

Once inside the rail station, the young duo, now kindred spirits as well as work colleagues, were set to go their separate ways as each was destined for different platforms.

"It has been real pleasure working under you today, instructor-san," said Ryuki with great sincerity. "Even in one day I have learned much. I just know you are destined for greater things."

"So, kind, Endo-san. I wish I could share your optimism. Unfortunately a frog in the smallest pond never knows the greatest lake."

The trainee stood directly in front of his mentor and, with his arms pressed to his sides, respected him with a deep *kerei* bow. "You can count on me to be there on time tomorrow, Osako-san."

"I know I can," replied Hiromi, his faith in people greatly restored. "See you in the morning, Endo-san."

*

Because of the CEO's impending visit, every member of the team made an extra effort to arrive early the next morning and all wore their best suits. Kitano paced the office nervously rehearsing a speech he had prepared while his subordinates got on with their work.

Hiromi and Ryuki surreptitiously watched their supervisor with keen interest. "He's like a cat on a hot tin roof," noted the trainee.

"Oh, you are going to see some serious toadying today," Hiromi replied, his tone mischievous.

"Do you really think that the big boss will fall for his act?" Ryuki asked.

"I sincerely doubt it, Endo-san. Mr Suzuki is an intelligent man who would see that Kitano is every bit as fake as his Rolex, but ultimately he judges people by their performance."

Ryuki pressed his lips together and kept his thoughts to himself.

The outgoing section manager burst from his private office to announce breathlessly that the CEO was about to arrive. He had already sent his secretary to the ground floor to be on hand to greet him. Kitano rushed to a window and caught a bird's eye view of the chief's Rolls Royce pulling up to the sidewalk. The CEO's chauffeur rushed to open the car door and bowed to Mr Suzuki as the great man exited the vehicle.

"He's on his way, he's on his way!" the supervisor squawked, flapping his arms as if he were about to take flight.

Yui Kishi spun in her chair and shot Kitano one of her scowls as the section manager trotted to the office's glass doors and wedged them open. He and Kitano stood near the doorway as rigidly as palace guards, their ridiculousness plain for all to see. The team stood as one to greet the big boss and bowed reverentially as he entered their office space.

"Please, everyone, have a seat," said Mr Suzuki with a benevolent smile.

The section manager was the first to address his superior. "Would you like a tea or coffee, Suzuki-san? I can ask one of the girls—"

"That won't be necessary," replied the CEO.

Bowing as if his worthless life depended on it, Kitano chipped in, "We already have the boardroom set up for you, Suzuki-san."

"Again, not necessary," said the big boss dismissively. "I thought I'd hold a meeting right here in front of the team."

"Whatever you say, Suzuki-san," the supervisor acquiesced.

The CEO stood at the end of a row of desks and took centre stage. "Gather around, everyone," he said with a good-natured smile. "I am the bearer of good news. I am here specifically to announce who is to be your new section manager."

The Leech licked his lips and struggled to contain his smile while the outgoing section manager unobtrusively patted him on the back. The hearts of everyone else sank.

An impish look bloomed on Mr Suzuki's face. "And I will leave it to my son to deliver the good news."

A moment of great confusion among those assembled gave rise to shared stupefaction as the new boy stepped forward from the huddle and stood shoulder to shoulder with the CEO. Hiromi's jaw almost dropped from its hinges as he struggled to make sense of this startling development.

The room fell silent and Ryuki gently cleared his throat. "Good morning, everyone. My real name is

Ryuki Suzuki. My father sent me here yesterday to work undercover because he had suspicions that the right people weren't getting the recognition they deserved."

This revelation set off a susurration of whispers. The Leech felt sick to his stomach and started to shrink into his cheap suit.

Ryuki continued, his tone authoritative. "I would like to thank Osako-san for opening my eyes to what has really been going on in this workplace. He has a clear understanding of our company's vision while you, Kitano-san, are little more than a chauvinist and a parasite."

There was a collective gasp. Yui Kishi's scowl turned into a feline smile.

Mr Suzuki senior took over the reins. "Kitano-san, I expect you to tender your resignation with immediate effect. Failure to do so will lead me to make your life very difficult very quickly."

All eyes were on The Leech as he staggered backwards from the volley of Mr Suzuki's words.

"And that brings me to the good news," the CEO resumed, smiling at Hiromi. "I name Osako-san as your new section manager and Kishi-san your supervisor."

Dorothy in Oz

"Here's your lemonade, Dorothy," said the nice lady. "Now why don't you tell me all about this amazing trip you had."

I reached for the glass, took a sip and set it down on a side table, keen to tell this grown-up all about my epic adventure. The likeable lady had introduced herself as Mrs Russell and seemed prepared to believe my bizarre story when others hadn't.

"It was when that recent cyclone swept in across the prairie," I began, hitching up my white socks and allowing myself to get comfortable in the chair. "The sky turned dark and Uncle Henry burst into the house, warning us that it was going to be a bad one. Aunt Em got into a panic and screamed for us to run for the cellar."

"Very wise," said Mrs Russell, listening to me intently while drinking her coffee.

"So I grabbed hold of poor Toto, who was terribly scared as you can imagine—"

"Toto is your dog, I assume?" asked the lady.

"Oh yes, he's a sweet little thing," I replied. "But

before we could get to the cellar the cyclone lifted the house up in the air and took it high up into the clouds as if it were as light as a feather."

I could see that Mrs Russell was astonished but she hadn't heard the half of it. I couldn't wait to tell her the rest.

"We were tossed around like a boat in a storm for ages. Even so, I managed to fall asleep."

I saw that Mrs Russell was surprised by what I had just said.

"You fell asleep, even though your house was being buffeted about up in the sky?" she asked.

"Yes. And when I woke, the house stood in another world that certainly wasn't Kansas. I looked through a window expecting to see the prairie but instead there were green fields, babbling brooks and beautiful flowers. Oh, you should have seen it, Mrs Russell."

"I'm trying to picture it, Dorothy," she replied.

Excited that my story was being heard, I spoke quickly, wanting to get to the best parts. "Then all of a sudden we were surrounded by these queer little creatures. Men and women, all older than you, Mrs Russell, but none of them any taller than a child."

"Astonishing," she said, looking suitably fascinated.

"They were called Munchkins, and some of them had little bells on their hats that tinkled as they walked," I explained.

"So what happened next, Dorothy?" enquired Mrs Russell.

"Well, as if things weren't already out of the ordinary,

I met a friendly witch who gave me some magical shoes and told me to follow a yellow brick road that would lead me to a wizard who lived in the Emerald City."

I paused for breath, thrilled that Mrs Russell was taking my story seriously. The person I had spoken to earlier had told me that I was talking nonsense and had made the whole thing up. That had made me very cross indeed.

"Go on," Mrs Russell urged.

I was greatly reassured by this lady's kind tone and didn't feel at all reluctant to reveal more of my peculiar story. "As I followed this yellow brick road, Mrs Russell, I happened upon a scarecrow. He spoke to me as if it were a perfectly normal thing for a scarecrow to do."

I paused to gauge the reaction on her face. As I had expected, she was astonished. "A talking scarecrow?" she gasped, leaning in closer.

"Yes. And he needed a brain so I told him that the wizard might be able to find him one."

Just as I was warming to the task, another lady interrupted our conversation to give Mrs Russell some papers to sign.

"I'm sorry about that, Dorothy," Mrs Russell said. "Please continue."

"So the scarecrow joined me and Toto on the road until we met a tin man who needed a heart and a cowardly lion who had lost his nerve. We all needed something, Mrs Russell."

Mrs Russell looked perplexed. "So what was it that *you* needed, Dorothy?"

"To get back here to Kansas, of course," I replied. "You see, there's no place like home."

I heard familiar voices behind me. Mrs Russell looked up. When I turned my head, I couldn't believe my eyes. Padding towards us, with his tail draped over one arm, was the cowardly lion. Clanking alongside him was the heartless tin man, and bringing up the rear was the brainless one, the scarecrow.

"Here they are, Mrs Russell!" I enthused. "These are the three good friends I was telling you about. The ones I met on the yellow brick road!"

*

Dorothy's three sons milled around the communal living room of the care home in Manchester, not quite knowing what to do or say. "How has she been?" enquired the brainless one.

"She's been fine, haven't you, Dorothy?" replied Mrs Russell, touching the old lady's knee. "Your mum's been telling me all about her trip to the Land of Oz again."

The Sacred Lake

Boufa, Africa, in the seventeenth century

With the benefit of hindsight Abu Sidibé, also known as Abu the Dreamer, often rued an opportunity he had once declined. At the age of sixteen he had been offered an apprenticeship by Mr Akombi, the respected local silversmith. Instead, Abu had honoured his father's wish for him to take over the family's postage stamp of land; since then he had grown maize and kept scraggy goats for thirty meagre years.

To make matters worse Youssef Dabo, the boy who had taken the apprenticeship in his place, went on to become a silver trader who swanned around the village in fine clothes and jewellery while Abu and his wife had to eke out a paltry existence. Though Abu's wife, Fatouma, was content to till the land and milk goats, her husband dreamed of a life that didn't involve blood, sweat and toil.

Local folklore told of Zilawi, a not-too-distant village that existed in a fertile patch of the Saharan desert. It was whispered that Zilawi was sited next to a sacred lake that could restore the old to younger versions of themselves. Sidibé, now that he was aged forty-six, was aching to try it out for himself.

"We are not getting any younger, Fatouma," Abu grumbled, leaning his bony arms on a hoe. "And we do not have a son or a daughter to help us. This sacred lake is said to have magical properties. You and I can be young again. We could start afresh."

His wife was far from convinced. "Fools say a lot of things, Abu. How is it that we have never met one person who has visited this place?"

"Because it must be so wonderful that once a person has seen its splendour and bathed in its lake they never leave."

Fatouma tightened her headscarf. "You are depending on hearsay, husband. For all we know, this place might not even exist."

As Abu was so intent on going there her words stung. "It exists, Fatouma. How can you say such a thing?"

"I say it because you are basing this solely on folklore passed down by word of mouth. No wonder they call you Abu the Dreamer." Fatouma released a deep sigh and returned to hacking at the dry soil with her hoe, hoping that her husband would do likewise.

"I am not going to give up on my dream, Fatouma," he vowed. "We cannot continue to live like peasants, working the land until we are too old to move. In time you will come to see that this sacred lake shall be our salvation."

*

The driving motivation behind Abu's eagerness was his desire to relive past glories. For a teenage boy from humble beginnings to being able to own a modest plot of land and a few goats was something he had once been proud of. "You are born to do this, son, and one day will become a great farmer," his father had foretold. "I ask you this: if wet clay was placed in every man's hand, could they all become potters?"

With his new bride by his side, Abu and Fatouma had been the dream team of their day. At that time Fatouma was the prettiest girl in the village, with silky skin and a smile that could charm birds from the trees. Even now, despite her face being wrinkled from three decades of toiling in the sun, she remained beautiful and carried herself with effortless grace.

By way of contrast, Abu was not especially handsome. He was tall and wiry, with the eyes of a tortoise and teeth that wouldn't have looked out of place on a camel. But what Abu Sidibé lacked in looks he made up for in character. He was known locally as a reliable individual who made a virtue out of doing good unto others while expecting nothing in return. Unfortunately he was also something of a fantasist, prepared to believe almost anything that fortified his pipe dreams.

Sitting in the shade of an almond tree and whistling a thin tune, Abu obligingly peeled a mango for his wife. She could tell by his obsequious demeanour that he was about to launch yet another bid to cajole her into joining him on his absurd quest. Browbeaten almost to the point of submission, she waved off a fly and awaited his next move.

"Here is your juicy mango, my beloved," Abu cooed, passing her a large slice. "I have also brought water for when your hands become sticky."

Fatouma accepted the fruit and eyed him with acute suspicion. "Just say what you want to say, husband. I am too old for games."

Abu looked at his wife guardedly. "A prophet came to me in a dream last night," he lied, hoping that divine instruction might further his cause. "He told me about the sacred lake and said that it was our destiny to bathe in its magical waters. He promised that we would be teenagers again."

Fatouma immediately suspected that he was making up the story. "Did he also remind you that your wife is not stupid, Abu?"

"No, I distinctly recall him focussing more on the lake," he replied, unable to maintain eye contact.

Fatouma finished her slice of mango, sucked on her fingertips and poured water over her hands. "Fine, Abu. Have it your way. We will look for your precious lake," she said sturdily. "But if things start to get tough in the desert, we are turning back."

"A thousand thank yous, my love!" her husband enthused. "You have made me the happiest man in Boufa. God must have been very pleased with me the day he sent you!"

*

On the morning of Abu and Fatouma's departure,

the entire village gathered at their smallholding to see them off. The sun was still low in the sky, casting long shadows on the dusty ground as clouds of midges oscillated above the villagers' heads. Though the general consensus was one of supreme optimism, some of those present voiced their concerns freely.

"But we have such a beautiful lake here!" reasoned Touré the blacksmith, thinking that the couple needed their heads examined.

"Need I remind you, Touré, that the lake in Zilawi has magical properties?" replied Fakoly the potter, inducing murmurs of approval.

"And let us not forget that a prophet told Abu about the sacred lake in a dream!" shouted Fatouma's sister, raising an index finger to the sky and prompting a ripple of oohs and aahs throughout the crowd.

"This is insane! We don't even know if there *is* a lake," the blacksmith cautioned. "Not one of us has dipped our toes in it or even set eyes on it. These good people are risking everything on a legend."

"I agree," said Oumar the cattle farmer. "For all we know, Zilawi might only be a figment of someone's imagination."

Because the prevailing mood was buoyant, the two dissenters were shouted down and ridiculed for their pessimism. Abu was called upon to make a speech and stood atop a sawn tree stump so he could be seen by all. "Dear friends," he began, his camel teeth as white as his turban. "I completely understand why some of you are apprehensive but a man will discover more about himself if he takes a risk than if he plays it safe."

"Fortune favours the brave!" roared Fakoly, waving a rattan in the air, triggering a chain reaction of men whooping and brandishing their canes.

"I suppose that we may never see you two again after today," ventured the village elder mournfully.

Abu's eyes twinkled. "If you do, we will appear before you as teenagers and our bones won't creak when we walk!"

This assertion provoked a raucous cheer from his thrilled audience and prompted many to wish they had such courage.

"My dear friends, the time has come to say goodbye," declared Abu the Dreamer, at which point he and Fatouma were engulfed in a tide of hugs and kisses.

The farmer, having entrusted the running of his land to Ikemba, his favourite cousin, slapped the dry mud walls of his home and bade it farewell. He and Fatouma had bought a pack horse for the journey and filled its saddlebags with dates, cheese and dried meat. More importantly, the beast was burdened with water-filled earthenware pots, enough to last four days. The intrepid duo set off for the desert to a trill of jubilant cheers and whistles.

Abu was filled with enthusiasm and walked with his head held high. In contrast, having said goodbye to friends and family Fatouma was inconsolable. Even their scraggy goats were sad to see them depart and sent them on their way with a chorus of forlorn bleats.

The blacksmith's daughter walked by with her baby

swathed in cloth and tied to her back, a sight that reaffirmed to Abu how wonderful it was to be young. "See, Fatouma," he said, flourishing an arm as if casting seed. "The young have their lives ahead of them, whereas our best years are behind us. You will thank me for my great wisdom when we are young again."

Fatouma tucked a wisp of hair under her headscarf and concentrated on putting one foot in front of the other.

*

Once they had reached the edge of the Saharan desert, Fatouma took one last lingering look at the village of Boufa and its beautiful lake. Her fear was that she would never return. For the love of her husband she kept her thoughts to herself and continued to walk. Ahead of them was a seemingly endless universe of sand and sky.

*

After making good progress, Abu was already imagining himself young and virile again, a master of his own destiny. Stopping frequently to slake their thirst, it didn't take long for them to stumble upon a group of nomadic merchants. Dressed in black robes, they resembled a parliament of crows as they perched on a patterned blanket beside a caravan of kneeling camels.

"*Salaam alaikum!*" the tribesmen greeted
"*Wa-alaikum-assalaam!*" Abu responded.

The nomads, astonished to see two people alone in the desert, were naturally curious. "*Effendi,* are you intending to travel far?" their leader asked Abu.

"To Zilawi," the farmer replied proudly. "Have you been there, my friend?"

"I have heard of this place," replied the elder, glancing at his entourage, "but I have not seen it. It is said to be north of here, maybe two days on foot."

"Then we should leave you in peace and be on our way," said Abu, distracted by the sight of mint tea being poured into glasses from an Arabic teapot.

"Come," beckoned the leader, with a Sphinx-like smile. "You must drink with us before you continue on your ambitious journey."

Several hours after saying goodbye to the nomads and thanking them for their hospitality, Abu and Fatouma floundered in the heat and walked as if their sandals were made from broken glass. The horse fared no better and struggled with its load on the soft sand. Tracking the sun, Abu knew in which direction they should proceed but had no idea of the distance. By nightfall the couple were exhausted and stopped for food and water before falling asleep under the stars. The temperature dropped dramatically and they woke cold and shivering.

Abu unilaterally decided that they should continue their odyssey in the dark. Following the North Star, the couple resumed their trek until dawn broke on the horizon. They were initially heartened by their progress but the unforgiving heat was soon upon them and their feet became terribly blistered. To make matters worse, instead of the flat surface they had become accustomed to, ahead of them appeared wave after wave of steep-sided dunes.

"Our horse will not be able to climb over those," said Fatouma despondently.

"He will," replied Abu with his usual optimism. "Have faith, my love. We might make Zilawi by nightfall if we press on."

Fatouma ran a sleeve across her sweaty forehead and took several glugs of water. Wincing behind the headscarf that covered her face, she proceeded with grim determination.

Scaling just one of the dunes took almost all of their energy and the duo collapsed in a state of fatigue at its summit. "Look! Look!" shouted Abu huskily through cracked lips. "No more dunes, Fatouma. Our journey will be easier."

While struggling to negotiate the soft sand of the ridge, the couple had drunk more water than they had intended. After scuffing down the powdery incline to reach terra firma, Abu took stock of their rations. "Only two pots left," he announced, putting on a brave face.

"Two pots will not be enough," wailed Fatouma.

"It is enough for one day," her husband replied. "And, as God is my witness, we will reach Zilawi before very long."

*

Hours later, the sky darkened and veiled the sun. A

powerful tempest tore across the desert, bringing a violent sandstorm that stung their faces and knocked them off their feet. The couple lay face down on the ground and held tightly onto each other as they were sandblasted by the wind. No sooner had the storm passed than the sky was blue again, the heat once more scorching their throats. Alarmingly, their horse was showing signs of severe distress and had begun to breathe heavily.

"He needs water," said Fatouma, stroking the horse's flank.

"So do we," replied Abu, spitting sand from his dry mouth. "And our need is greater than his, I'm afraid."

"Just a little. It's too cruel. Please, Abu."

With great misgivings, her husband relented and gave the horse water, secretly praying to God that they would soon reach Zilawi. Because of his exhaustion the pot slipped from Abu's grasp and smashed on the ground, spilling its entire load into the sand.

"No-o! I cannot believe my eyes!" shrilled Fatouma. "Look what you did! Now we are going to die alone out here in this wilderness!"

Though he was inwardly terrified, Abu sought to quell his wife's fears. "Relax. We still have one more," he said, dizzy from dehydration. "We are almost there, my love. I can smell it in the air."

Without warning, the horse let out a stricken roar and collapsed to the ground dead, crushing the last remaining water pot beneath it. The sun continued to blaze ferociously. The need for Abu and Fatouma to keep moving forward had become an immediate matter of life or death.

*

After two hours of hard slog, delirium had set in and their bodies were at the limits of endurance. Having fainted for a third time, Fatouma remained on the ground ready to give up. "I cannot go any further," she rasped through blistered lips. "I am at God's mercy and happy to die."

Squinting through tired eyes, Abu saw a mirage in the mid-distance. Shimmering like a sheet of silver in the sun's furnace, he could make out the surface of a lake.

"Fatouma! Fatouma! Wake up!" he croaked, trying to revive his dying wife. "Use whatever strength you have left, my love! We are nearly there!"

Drawing power from deep within, Fatouma rose to her feet and, guided by Abu's arm, trudged forward blindly on uncertain legs. Almost a ghost, she drifted into a joyous memory of her father tying a cotton string to her waist on the day she was married.

After a superhuman effort, they succeeded in dragging their bodies to the lake. Abu immediately immersed himself into its shallows and drank of its water then dribbled some into Fatouma's mouth from cupped hands. Despair turned to jubilation and the farmer whooped for joy as his darling opened her beautiful eyes and managed a weak smile.

"Yes! Yes! By the will of God we have made it!" he

shouted, splashing water onto his beloved to cool her down.

Shuffling by the water's edge, an elderly local from the village of Zilawi was most intrigued to see an exultant stranger causing such a commotion.

"*Salaam alaikum,*" said the old man warmly. "I know everyone in these parts but I cannot place either of you. Where are you from, my friends?"

"We are from Boufa!" replied Abu joyously, wondering when the lake's magical powers would begin to take effect.

"Ah, Boufa!" the resident enthused, his eyes shining like wet pebbles. "The village that is said to have a sacred lake."

The Pot of Gold

Mr Kenneth Fitzpatrick, an Irishman with neither friends nor a kind bone in his body, stood on the flagstone floor of his farmhouse kitchen barking orders at his long-suffering wife, despite her occupying an entirely different room. "Orla! Have you prepared me a packed lunch or not, woman?"

His wife clumped into the kitchen and scorched him with her green eyes. "For the love of God, Kenneth, would you stop it now? It's right there in front of you, if you'd even cared to look." With that, she picked up a crammed Tupperware container that sat no more than an arm's length from his fingertips and shoved it into his chest.

Fitzpatrick remained impenitent. "Well, it should be in plain view, woman. That way I'd have seen the fecking thing."

"How much plainer could it have been?" Orla snapped. "Perhaps I should place a little flag on top of it next time? Or circle it with a garland of flowers?"

Kenneth's eyes narrowed. "If only I had listened to my dear sainted mother when she said that I could have done better than you," he snorted.

"Well now, couldn't we all?" his wife retorted, putting her hands to her hips. "I could have married Dermot O'Donnell. Now there's a man."

Genial Dermot O'Donnell owned the neighbouring farm and any mention of his name drove Fitzpatrick into a fit of jealous rage. "What, with himself smiling all day long like a ventriloquist's dummy? Jaysus, the two of you would have made a right couple," he grouched.

"He's a kind, selfless soul, so he is. You could learn a lot from him, you ape."

Kenneth's nostrils flared. "That eejit has nothing that I haven't got. In fact, my land is a fair bit bigger than his. God, it must make him burn with envy."

"A man isn't judged by the size of his land," said Orla, with a sinful smile. "And he's not the sort to be envious."

"Ah, to hell with you, woman! I'm off!"

"He's the better man and you know it!" Fitzpatrick's wife shouted as he slammed the door behind him.

*

With the crops already harvested and fields laid bare, Fitzpatrick took to trimming the hedgerows, his mood no less foul than when he had left the house. A white horse clip-clopped along an adjacent bridleway and was brought to a halt by its rider. High in his saddle, and looking heroic in the morning sun, sat Dermot O'Donnell, who had stopped to wish his misanthropic neighbour a cheery good morning.

"What's good about it?" growled Fitzpatrick, folding his arms.

"Is this not God's own country, Kenneth?" said O'Donnell, his smile as wide as the River Shannon. "What's not to like, my friend?"

"I'm not your fecking friend, you grinning gobshite."

"Am I not?" replied Dermot, winking at his neighbour while commanding his horse to walk on. "Wishing you the loveliest of days, Kenneth."

"May your horse throw you into a fecking ditch, you arse!"

*

Much later, when hunger struck him, Fitzpatrick took off his wide-brimmed hat, sat with legs dangling from the tailgate of his Land Rover and unpeeled the Tupperware lid. Inside was a two-storey stack of sandwiches cut into triangles, along with a bag of cheese-and-onion crisps and a Mars bar. He cautiously lifted a corner of one sandwich in the way that an explosives expert checks a rucksack. "Ham and mustard again," he muttered to himself. "Always ham and fecking mustard."

Just as he was unscrewing the lid from his Thermos flask, Fitzpatrick heard a distinct tap-tap-tapping noise emanating from the hedge. Intrigued, he slid from the tailgate, got down on his knees and had a rummage, pushing leaves and branches aside to gain a clearer view. The noise remained clear and, to the farmer's sheer amazement, there sat a tiny man no bigger than his hand. The little man wore a buckled top hat and a green suit sullied with dirt. He was so busy hammering tacks into leather and making a pair of shoes for himself that he failed to notice a huge face gawping in at him.

If Fitzpatrick hadn't seen the wee man with his own eyes, he would never have believed it. He thought leprechauns only existed in folklore or in the addled minds of old drunks spinning yarns for free beer. Legend had it that great riches awaited anyone who could successfully hold the gaze of such a creature, so the farmer watched the little man as keenly as a cat watches a goldfish.

"Hello, little fella," said Fitzpatrick, catching the leprechaun's attention.

"Good day to you, sir," replied the tiny man nonchalantly. "Begorrah, would you look at the size of your giant head!"

"Never mind the size of my head, you imp. So long as I keep you in my sight you have to give me a pot of gold."

"Do I now?" replied the leprechaun, stroking his carroty beard. "Now where did you hear that?"

"Everyone in Ireland knows it to be true," the farmer smirked. "You lot have it buried at the end of a rainbow and I claim it as mine."

"Jaysus, away with you, sir!" retorted the leprechaun, waving his tiny hammer. "How the devil would you get to the end of a rainbow?"

"I'm not giving up on this, you wee rascal. And I

want what's due." Fitzpatrick kept his eyes fixed on the creature, knowing that it would vanish in a flash if his gaze slipped.

"Look! If it isn't St Brendan, himself!" shouted the leprechaun, pointing over the farmer's shoulder.

Kenneth didn't flinch. "I'm not falling for your tricks, you little shit. Now take me to this pot of gold."

"Fair enough, sir. I can see that I have met my match. You are by far the most intelligent mortal I've yet clapped eyes on."

This statement made Fitzpatrick feel very good indeed. Apart from those he gave himself, he wasn't used to compliments. "Now you're talking, boyo," he said, almost cross-eyed from staring. "So you'll be showing me that pot of gold then?"

"Of course, sir," replied the leprechaun compliantly. "It is but a few fields yonder."

"On my land, I hope?" asked the farmer, a little panicked.

"Yes, for sure it's on your land."

The short journey was a clumsy one due to Fitzpatrick having to maintain eye contact with the leprechaun as the little man sat on the palm of his hand. The farmer stumbled on rocks, traversed ditches and jostled through gaps in hedges, never once taking his eyes off the tiny creature.

"Not far to go now," said the leprechaun with an impish grin, his eyes gleaming like well-cut jewels. "You're doing just grand, sir."

He guided the farmer to a spot in the centre of a

ploughed field and declared that the pot of gold was buried where he stood.

"Now you wouldn't be trying to trick me, would you, you little devil?" asked Fitzpatrick, keeping the leprechaun where he could see him.

"May the Lord God Almighty strike me down if I'm lying," replied the little man. "It's buried right there under your boots. We stole it from the Vikings when they invaded Ireland in the eighth century."

Despite not knowing if he should take the leprechaun at his word, Kenneth arrived at the realisation that he needed to fetch a spade from his garage. To drive his Land Rover while continuing to keep an eye on his captive was unfeasible. "With you gone, how in God's name would I find this spot again?" asked the farmer.

"Jaysus, I'm deeply surprised at you, sir," replied the leprechaun, reclining on Fitzpatrick's calloused hand. "It seems obvious to me that you should place that broad hat of yours on the soil, sir. X marks the spot, so to speak."

Kenneth narrowed his eyes. "Look, I'm not an eejit, you little maggot. What if a gust of wind were to blow it away?"

"It wouldn't blow away if you were to weigh it down with that fat belt of yours, now would it?" replied the leprechaun with a sly smile.

"Brilliant! That is exactly what I shall do!" exclaimed the farmer, delighted with what he'd accomplished so far. "I've heard it said many times that you imps always get one over on us humans but you'd have to get up pretty early in the morning to hoodwink me, you wee trickster."

The leprechaun adopted a subdued countenance. "As I said, sir, you are truly the most intelligent mortal that I have come across. So, am I free to go now?"

"You are, you little fecker. But God help you if you've lied to me."

"I'm as true as the sky, sir."

"Go on, scram," said Fitzpatrick, removing his hat and unfastening his belt. The little man disappeared and all that trailed behind him was his mischievous giggle.

*

When the farmer returned with a spade, his heavy belt was nowhere to be seen. The leprechaun had pilfered it, intending to make several pairs of brogues from its leather. And Fitzpatrick's hat, caught by the wind, was dancing all around the field.

*

Some weeks later…

Dermot O'Donnell had dropped his wife off earlier at the train station in Ballyhale and was walking his black Labrador along the bridleway at the edge of his farm.

"What have you found there, Guinness?" he asked his dog as he keenly investigated something in the hawthorn hedge that flanked the track. All he could see of Guinness was his hindquarters and wagging tail.

"Wrruff!" barked his dog, as if to say 'come and look at this'.

Dermot got down onto his hands and knees. "What am I supposed to be looking for?" he asked rhetorically.

With his head now inside the hedge, and with Guinness pawing at his back, the farmer felt sure he could hear a creature whimpering as if in great pain. To Dermot's complete astonishment, a tiny man lay on the leafy ground dressed all in green, his ankle caught in a mousetrap.

"Sacred Jesus, it's a leprechaun!" O'Donnell gasped. Until her dying day, his grandmother had insisted she had seen one and not one person had believed her.

"O cruel human. If you've come to kill me then make it quick," whined the imp. "My leg's banjaxed and I'm in terrible pain, so I am."

"Kill you? Dear God, no," replied Dermot, appalled by the thought. "Here, little fella, let me spring you from that." As O'Donnell reached in, he saw a profusion of mousetraps on the mulchy ground. *That spiteful maggot,* he thought to himself, knowing that Fitzpatrick had set them there for some vindictive reason.

Once the farmer had released the jaws of the trap, the relief on the leprechaun's face was palpable. "I am indebted to you, sir," he said, rubbing his damaged leg. "To be sure, that other farmer has it in for me since I had my fun with him."

Despite his incredulity at what he was witnessing, this statement caused O'Donnell to smile broadly. "So what kind of fun did you have with the auld bugger?" he enquired, lifting the leprechaun gently from the hedge and laying him on the grass verge, inducing a robin to flitter down to see what all the fuss was about.

"Well, sir, although I found him to be a most undeserving soul, I was forced to tell him where a pot of gold was buried in that field yonder."

"So now I'm guessing that the gold wasn't there," said Dermot, his smile growing wider.

"Oh, it was there all right," replied the little man, stifling a giggle, "but we wasted no time reclaiming it before the devil could get his greedy hands on it."

"Honest to God, that's the funniest thing I've heard in ages," the farmer chuckled. "Now I know why he spent a week digging up the whole blessed field with a JCB."

"We thought it was funny too," the leprechaun agreed, straightening his green hat and feeling rather pleased with himself. "I doubt that even the sea would give that misery a wave."

O'Donnell was in full agreement. "Sure, he's a bad article, that one."

The wee man dropped his easy smile and scrutinised the human with sudden mistrust. "No doubt you'll be wanting all the gold for yourself now, sir?"

"I have no interest in your pot of gold," replied Dermot with great sincerity. "I'd sooner have a cup of tea than a pot of gold."

The leprechaun was startled by the farmer's assertion. He had never encountered a human before who wasn't consumed by greed. "You would deny yourself such riches, sir?"

"Fortune has already favoured me, my little friend," explained Dermot, getting on his haunches to converse more intimately. "You see, I have all that I need in life. A wonderful wife, first-rate friends, a farm that gives me a decent living and my good health. What more could a fella need?"

After gaping at the farmer in astonishment for several seconds, the leprechaun struggled to his feet. "Jaysus, Mary and Joseph, I'll be walking with a limp for a fair while," he winced, only for the dog to lick his face and send him tumbling back down again.

"Come, let me take you to my house, my tiny friend," Dermot smiled. "I'll fix that leg up for you so you'll be able to walk just grand."

The leprechaun, who had never thought to trust a mortal before, allowed himself to be carried in the farmer's shirt pocket. He didn't care to vanish, despite having every opportunity. "Sure, but it's a grand view from up here!" he enthused.

Guinness padded alongside, unsurprised that his master would want to take such an exotic creature home with him.

"Here we are," said the farmer after the two-mile walk, removing his green wellingtons in the hallway.

"Jaysus, but it's hot in here," puffed the leprechaun loosening his collar. "Give me a rabbit hole or a nice hedge any day."

O'Donnell clicked off the central heating and transported his little guest to the kitchen where he sat him upon a marble worktop.

"Now where would that fine wife of yours be?" asked the little man.

"You know my wife?" asked Dermot.

"I've seen her around."

"She's visiting her sister in Dublin for a few days."

"A fine woman, if you don't mind me saying. I'd climb up her legs, so I would."

The farmer laughed heartily. "You're a wee rascal, for sure."

O'Donnell carefully rolled up the leprechaun's trouser leg. The little man had sustained a nasty gash but, despite there being a deep dent across his shin, nothing appeared to be broken. "I'll fetch some antiseptic cream and make you a little bandage. In the meantime, could I offer you a thimble of tea or a saucer of water?"

"I wouldn't say no to a pint of the black stuff," said the leprechaun without delay.

"Oh boy," chuckled Dermot. "With the size of you, I'm not sure you could handle a whole pint of stout."

"I'll have a good go," replied the wee man. "Just pour it into the dog bowl, sir, and I'll drink from that."

By the time O'Donnell had returned with a bandage cut to size and a walking stick fashioned from a clothes peg, his houseguest was propped against the dog bowl with a gap-toothed smile across his rosy-cheeked face. "Jaysus, that tasted good. And honest to God, my leg feels better as a result."

While the farmer treated the little man's leg, they discussed the detrimental effect that the removal of many of the country's hedgerows was having on the plant and animal species that thrived in them. "Not only that," slurred the leprechaun. "What would my kind do without hedges? Christ, you humans have a lot to answer for."

Dermot pondered this for a few seconds and a lightbulb moment of inspiration illuminated his brain. "My friend, does your offer of a pot of gold still stand?"

"It does," answered the imp.

"Then I think I can put it to good use."

*

"I guess I ought to get you back to your hedge, my man," suggested the farmer some hours later, rattling his car keys.

"You'll not be needing those," replied the leprechaun using his makeshift crutch to hobble into the hallway. "You see, I have my own means of transport."

The little fellow clambered down onto the front doorstep then shoved two fingers in his mouth and issued an ear-splitting whistle. Within a matter of seconds a mouse, harnessed in riding tack, streaked to where they stood.

"Jeez, now would you look at that?" gasped O'Donnell, marvelling at the rodent's rudimentary bridle, saddle, reins and stirrups, all fashioned from leather belts and shoelaces.

"My chariot awaits, and he can run like the wind," said the leprechaun, as he climbed on top of the rodent.

"Giddy up, mousey!"

And with that, the little man was hurtling out of the farmyard like a champion jockey.

*

One month later...

It surprised Kenneth Fitzpatrick greatly when one day he noticed Dermot O'Donnell chugging majestically along the bridleway in a brand new, top-of-the-range Massey Ferguson tractor.

"How the feck can that shitehawk afford *that?*" he groused, envy leaking from every pore. Then, to further his astonishment, a convoy of lorries pulled up onto the verges. From them appeared a gang of labourers, each carrying a bundle of young hawthorn plants.

Once he was within earshot, Fitzpatrick called over to his neighbour. "Hey, O'Donnell! You're spending money like it's going out of fashion. What in God's name are you doing there?"

"Oh, I've decided for ecological reasons to plant new hedgerows inside all of the existing ones."

"Have you gone completely fecking mad, you eejit? You do know you'll be cutting into your profits for the sake of a few birds, flowers and insects?"

"I do."

"Jaysus, you're not the full shilling, man."

"Perhaps not, Kenneth."

"Flash new tractor as well. You seem to be doing well

245

for yourself. Must have cost a small fortune."

"Yes, yes it did. But such is life."

"Then again, O'Donnell. With you thinking you're all high and mighty now, let's not forget that my land is a fair bit bigger than yours."

"So it is," smiled Dermot.

Waiting for Ryan

Phuket, Thailand 2004

Mishti Kapur was listening to American pop music through in-ear headphones on a shaded sun lounger while her fatigued parents slept beside her. Though they had flown first class from Mumbai to Bangkok, her family were initially forced to endure a six-hour delay at their home city's international airport. Adding to their misfortune, they had missed their connecting flight to Phuket and arrived on the island minus one Gucci suitcase.

Mishti's parents, part of Mumbai's burgeoning elite, had also brought along Geeta, their son's nanny, who had travelled separately in economy class. Mishti, who had recently turned sixteen, adored Geeta for the latter was formerly her childhood nanny, a compliant woman whose love for her charges was unstinting and infinite.

Mishti's five-year-old brother, Sachin, was gleefully splashing about in the children's pool while Geeta chaperoned him from the water's edge. "Mishti! Please come play!" Sachin shouted, the widest of grins lighting up his face.

Mishti simply acknowledged him with a cheery wave and continued to sip iced lemon tea through a straw.

Just then, he appeared on her radar again: a handsome blond-haired boy of a similar age who had gazed audaciously in her direction a few times. His interest was as unmistakable as it was unexpected. Slim and athletic in red swim shorts, he exuded an air of confidence; each time he flashed Mishti a smile it caused her heart to flutter.

Not accustomed to such bravado, she maintained an air of aloofness behind her oversized sunglasses, pretending that she hadn't seen him. It amused her that the teenager soon abandoned his casual overtures when the man pushing the ice-cream cart appeared in the mid-distance. She watched the soles of his feet blur as he scampered off in its direction. *That boy has the attention span of a goldfish*, she smiled to herself.

Mishti stretched cat-like and released a sigh of satisfaction. The Redford Patong Beach Resort had beguiled her the moment she had first set eyes on its tropical gardens and the sea beyond. The freeform swimming pool, ultramarine and inviting, beckoned her with its glittering dazzle, so Mishti slipped a kaftan over her swimsuit and padded to its edge where she sat with her legs dangling in the water.

The pretty teenager had pushed her shades to the top of her head and was tilting her face to the sun when a shadow, accompanied by an English accent, fell across her. "I bought you an ice cream," the voice chimed from above. "I hope you like coconut flavour."

She visored her eyes and squinted up at the boy who was holding two cones and grinning as if he were the bearer of promising news. "Um, thank you," she said, not sure how to react to this unanticipated gift and receiving it as if it were a live grenade.

"Budge up, I'll join you," he breezed, dipping his feet in the sparkling water and sitting close enough that his leg brushed against hers. Mishti looked behind her, worried what her parents might think. Luckily they were still dead to the world.

The boy nudged her with his elbow. "So, what's your name? Mine's Ryan."

"Mine's Mishti," she replied, dropping her sunglasses in an attempt to hide her nervousness.

"Beautiful name. I'm guessing you're from India?"

"Yes, from Mumbai actually," she replied, holding the cone daintily. "Have you been?"

"No, but my mum travelled through India on her gap year and hasn't stopped raving about it since."

Mishti was already comfortable in Ryan's company, charmed by his gregariousness and polite manner. "And you're clearly English. Do you visit Thailand often?"

"I've been coming here since I was a kid. With my mum and dad, of course." She followed his line of sight as he pointed over his shoulder. Two people, whom she took to be his mother and father, waved merrily from their sun loungers.

"Better eat that up before it melts," he chuckled, noticing that rivulets of coconut ice cream were running down her hand.

They sat in silence for a while, licking their ice creams in synchronisation and sculling their feet in the water. Each time his leg touched hers, Mishti fizzed with excitement. Ryan was so enamoured by the pretty Indian girl that he very nearly draped an arm across her shoulder. He hoped she would remove her sunglasses so he could gaze into her chocolaty eyes again.

"How old are you, Mishti?" he asked.

"Just turned sixteen. You?"

"Same. My birthday was last week, the 24th of July."

Mishti's mouth was agape. "Omigod! *My* birthday is also July the 24th!"

Ryan's ever-present smile grew wider as Mishti pushed her sunglasses to the top of her head again and stared at him in disbelief. "How random is that?" he chuckled. "Here we are, two strangers born on the exact same day, finding ourselves sitting together by a pool in Thailand."

"It's crazy," said Mishti, with a shake of her head.

"And did you know that you are the spitting image of Pocahontas?" he grinned, wiping sweat from his brow.

Mishti effected an expression of faux indignation and gave him a playful shove. "You think I look like a Disney character?"

"A very pretty Disney character," he beamed, nudging her leg with his knee. "Hey, are you hungry? We could eat at the poolside restaurant."

Mishti grew anxious and looked to where her mother and father were still sleeping like babies. "Er, I'm not so sure, Ryan. You would not believe how strict my parents are—"

"They're both asleep. And anyway, what's the worst they can do?"

"Um—"

Ryan took Mishti's hand and coaxed her to her feet. "It would be nice to get to know you and my parents won't mind me charging it to the room."

As Mishti stood opposite Ryan, an unstoppable feeling of love for him unfurled its wings. He was talking but she barely caught a word. His eyes were as blue as if they'd fallen from the sky and she imagined him being the first boy she would ever kiss.

"So what do you say, Mishti?"

As if rescued from a trance, Mishti was returned to physical existence. "Um, I guess it would be OK. Sure. Why not?"

"Great. Let me fetch my T-shirt and I'll be right back."

Mishti watched him dash off to his lounger and then checked to see what her parents were doing. She was relieved to note that they were unlikely to wake up any time soon.

Ryan returned wearing a Coldplay T-shirt and escorted Mishti to the poolside restaurant. They passed Geeta on the way; she raised her eyebrows and shot an approving smile.

"Mishti! Who is that boy?" shouted Sachin, up to his armpits in water.

"Never you mind," his sister replied.

*

The teenagers shared a Margherita pizza and became lost in conversation. Ryan rattled on about his love for skateboarding and football, while Mishti talked about her private education and dream of becoming a doctor. They found that, despite living a world apart, they had much in common: the same tastes in literature and music; a fondness for black-and-white movies, and an inclination to stay loyal to friends. *Are you even real?* she mused, falling in love for the first time in her young life.

Becoming less worried about what her parents might think, Mishti threw caution to the wind and agreed to accompany Ryan to the beach. Her need to be with him was made all the more acute when he revealed that these were the final few hours of his family's holiday. The two walked barefoot along a path that ran through a line of coconut trees and took a few steps down to the sandy beach. Ahead of them was the infinite shimmer of the Andaman Sea, pleated with exhausted waves that were about to collapse over the finishing line.

A Thai beach vendor of a similar age to theirs approached with a sunshine smile illuminating his brown face. "Oh, you'll like this little guy," said Ryan. "His name's Sawat."

"*Sawasdee kap, Khun* Ryan!" the vendor shouted, pressing his fingers into a *wai*.

Ryan's response impressed Mishti. "*Sawasdee kap, Khun* Sawat."

The Thai boy was instantly mischievous, as was his nature. "Oh, you have brought new frien'. Perhap' she your girlfrien', *na*?" His smile widened as Mishti covered her face in her hands and groaned with a mixture of delight and embarrassment.

"I wish!" Ryan chuckled. "Sawat, this is my new friend Mishti, from India. Mishti, this is Sawat."

"Pleased to meet you Sawat," said Mishti, shaking the boy's hand. Unbeknown to her, Ryan's heart was bursting with pride.

The vendor noticed the sparkle in his friend's eyes and sought to play Cupid. "But you two look so good together. If you not boyfrien' and girlfrien', then maybe can be."

A great sadness descended on Ryan as it suddenly dawned on him that he might never see this beautiful girl again after today. He held Mishti's hand and instead of flinching she gazed into his eyes with a longing that couldn't be repressed.

The spell was suddenly broken. Behind them, from the hotel perimeter, a man's voice rumbled like a storm cloud. "Mishti! What are you doing, child? We couldn't see you!"

Mishti released Ryan's hand as if it were radioactive. "I have to go," she whispered, her eyes doleful.

"Can I see you later before we have to leave?" asked Ryan, desperate not to lose his Pocahontas.

Her father's voice grew louder. "Mishti! I am calling you!"

"I – I'm not sure," Mishti faltered, caught in two minds. "I'll come back to the beach if I get the chance."

"That's great," Ryan enthused. "I'll look out for you.

You'd better go."

"I love you, Ryan." The words flew from Mishti's mouth like an escaped butterfly. Ryan's eyes were suddenly as big as saucers and Mishti wondered why she had said such a stupid thing.

"I love you too," he replied.

Her father's voice boomed. "Mishti!"

"I'm coming, Papa!"

Ryan and Sawat watched her scuttle back to her father, kicking up sand as she ran. "Her father very angry," said Sawat, stating the obvious.

"He is indeed," replied Ryan as Mishti was read the riot act.

*

Escorting his daughter back to their sun loungers, Mr Kapur scolded her as loudly as was socially acceptable while they passed a fleshy line-up of sweaty sunbathers. "What were you thinking, Mishti, disappearing without telling us?"

"But you were both asleep—"

"It should make no difference, child. Your mother and I were worried about you. Even Geeta didn't know where you were. Anything could have happened."

"I don't see why you should be worried. And anyway, I'm not a child."

"Well, until the day you marry you are a child to us. And who is this fellow anyway? You're not safe around foreign boys. Where is he from? Australia?"

"He's from England, Papa, and he's a perfect gentleman."

"England! They're the worst!"

They reached their towelled cluster of loungers and Mishti's mother, shaded by a large umbrella, looked mightily relieved to see that her daughter hadn't been murdered after all. "I found her with a boy, Aisha. An English boy at that."

"What did this dreadful boy do to you, my poor baby?"

Mishti wanted to scream with frustration. Her parents' cosseting was suffocating her. "He did nothing to me, Mama. He's a nice boy and I am *not* a baby. I'm sixteen years old."

"But how can you know anything of this fellow?" her father reasoned. "What is his family background? And those English boys don't know how to keep their *totos* in their pants."

"Papa! You are being disgusting," Mishti cringed.

"It's true," nodded Mrs Kapur. "Your Auntie Seema in Manchester told me as much."

Mishti's father remained resolute. "Well, you are not to leave our sight or go gallivanting with any hooligan English boys. Do you hear me?"

"But—"

"My word is final, Mishti!"

*

Two hours passed and Mishti realised that time was running out. While she was being guarded like a princess, the best that she and Ryan could manage was the sharing of inconspicuous glances from a safe distance. Then an opportunity presented itself: her parents needed to return to their suite so they could phone the airline for a progress report on their lost suitcase.

"We've told Geeta to keep an eye on you, Mishti," instructed her father, wagging a finger. "You are not to go anywhere, do you understand?"

"I understand perfectly, Papa."

No sooner had her parents disappeared from view than Mishti was off her lounger and slipping into flip-flops. Geeta fed her a go-get-him smile and asked Sachin if he could keep a secret, to which he nodded.

Ryan was on his feet the second he saw Mishti heading his way while his parents cracked playful jokes at his expense.

Without a word, the teenagers decamped to a secluded part of the beach. Ryan held a phone in his hand and asked for Mishti's number.

"My parents won't let me have a phone," she replied. "But you might be able to phone me *here*." She handed him a slip of paper upon which she'd written her school address. "You could certainly write to me. I would like that."

Ryan slid the paper into the pocket of his shorts. "I'll definitely keep in contact, Mishti. To tell the truth, I'm blown away by you."

Mishti almost burst into tears and couldn't stop herself

from standing on tiptoes and kissing him fully on the mouth. "Did I kiss properly?" she asked, after they had come up for air.

"Yeah, you kissed properly," he beamed, drawing her into a protective hug. "You kiss nice."

"Thank you. It's just that I've never kissed a boy before."

"Really? You want to try again?"

They kissed some more and remained in each other's arms, wishing that they could suspend time.

Tears formed in Mishti's eyes as she prepared to say her goodbye. "Did you mean it when you said you loved me?" she asked earnestly.

"Of course I meant it," Ryan replied sincerely. "And I will definitely keep in contact. I can't go through life without seeing you again."

Mishti's tears came and she held onto him as tight as she could, burrowing her head into his chest. "Promise me you'll keep in touch, Ryan."

"I promise."

"I don't want to go but I have to," she sobbed, wiping her eyes on the sleeve of her kaftan. "If we ever lose contact, for whatever reason, I will be visiting the Taj Mahal on my twenty-first birthday. It's something I've been planning for almost all my life. It would be amazing to share it with you."

Ryan was all smiles. "Count me in. We'll both be celebrating our twenty-first birthdays. And we've got plenty of time to sort the details out."

Mishti became insistent, not wanting the importance

of her words to be lost in this brief portion of time. "Yes, but if we *do* lose contact, I will be somewhere near the bench that your Princess Diana once sat upon. I'll be there waiting for you at twelve midday. It's very famous for that reason, you can Google it."

"Twelve o'clock. The bench that Princess Diana sat on. Got it."

"Promise me that you will write, Ryan?"

"I already did. Of course I'll write."

They kissed one last time and Mishti stepped back to admire her English prince, capturing his image in her mind. "Please don't follow me, Ryan. My parents might have returned."

"I'll stay right here," he said, grinning from ear to ear.

Mishti's tears came easily and she began to drift away. "I love you, Ryan."

"I love you too, Mishti. I'll write soon."

His words hung on the sea breeze as she left footprints in the soft sand and disappeared through the coconut trees.

*

While travelling with his parents in the taxi to Phuket International Airport, a lightning bolt of realisation shocked Ryan from a lovesick trance. He remembered hanging his swim shorts from the ribs of their umbrella to dry and had forgotten to retrieve them when they gathered their belongings. *Mishti's address!* he thought, panic rising in his soul. "Mum, Dad! I left my swim shorts back at the pool!"

"Well, it's a bit late now, Ryan, we're halfway to the airport," his father grumbled.

"But they had a very important note in them!" Ryan sputtered.

"What? A love letter from your little Indian girlfriend?" his mother teased.

"Her address," Ryan begged. "Can we go back? Please?"

His father looked over his shoulder from the passenger seat. "Son, we're not turning back just to get some girl's address. We're cutting it fine as it is."

Ryan looked to his mother, hoping she might intercede, but she just smiled and ruffled his hair, remembering the teenage crushes that had once sent her crying to her bedroom. Her son clutched his face in anguish as rats scrabbled in his stomach. He felt certain he would never see his Pocahontas again.

*

Five months later, Boxing Day morning saw Ryan's family transfixed by their TV screen, horrified at the breaking news that Phuket, among other places, had been hit by a devastating tsunami.

"Oh, dear God, that's *our* hotel," gasped Ryan's mother, holding her hand to her mouth in horror at the video they were witnessing.

"Please, no. Those poor people," said Ryan's father, moved to tears.

Ryan's first dumbstruck thought was for the safety of his Thai friend, Sawat, who would likely have been on that beach as the murderous wall of water thundered in.

"Oh, God, I hope little Sawat's OK," his mother croaked, reading her son's mind.

Because of the scale of the disaster it took two weeks and countless phone calls before they were able to receive third-party confirmation that Sawat had survived.

*

24th July, 2008

In their parallel universes, Mishti and Ryan continued to long for each other in the intervening four years, though neither could possibly know of the other's ongoing devotion. In the first year after their meeting, Mishti rushed to her school matron on a daily basis hoping that a letter postmarked from England might appear in her mail. She returned crestfallen on each occasion but, even now on her twentieth birthday, she refused to give up on her dream of one day being reunited with the boy who had stolen her heart.

Ryan's regret ran deep. Each time his family returned to Phuket, he hoped against hope that he might spot Mishti cooling her feet in the Redford's swimming pool. His swim shorts had never been handed in and the only thing he had to cling onto was Mishti's assurance that she would be at the Taj Mahal in 2009, at the time and location specified. He wondered how his Pocahontas would be celebrating her twentieth birthday today and hoped that she was thinking of him. One thing was certain: he was going to move Heaven and Earth to ensure that he joined Mishti in precisely one year's time, so that they could reunite for their twenty-first.

*

India, 24th July, 2009
Ryan and Mishti's twenty-first birthdays

After alighting from his early morning train at one of Agra's clamorous rail stations, Ryan ran a gauntlet of persistent beggars before stepping into the sweltering heat to bag a taxi that would take him to the Taj Mahal. The driver, after trying to sell him every tour in his directory, dropped Ryan off at the West Gate where he was met by a bustling tide of humanity. The ticket queues were lengthy and chaotic but time was on Ryan's side.

*

Mishti and her two best friends were en route to Agra in a chauffeured limousine procured for her twenty-first birthday by her father. The journey was long and they'd stayed overnight at the Marriott in Bhopal. She had dreamily told Alisha and Zara of the possibility that her handsome beau from five years ago might make a sensational appearance. Despite thinking this to be fanciful in the extreme, her companions entertained her pipe dream and allowed their imaginations to run wild.

"If he is as dashing as you say, Mishti, I hope he brings a friend," Alisha gushed.

"Yum! Make that two friends," Zara giggled.

Sixty miles from Agra, disaster struck. A high-speed blowout sent the vehicle careening across the motorway. The chauffeur wrestled with the steering wheel and the girls screamed in terror.

After colliding violently with a truck, the limousine turned over and came to rest upside down with its wheels still spinning furiously. Of its four occupants only Mishti, with her pelvis and right leg broken, survived.

*

With plenty of time to spare before the noon deadline, Ryan identified the marble bench that was once graced by Princess Diana and felt a great sense of achievement that his meticulous planning had put him right where he needed to be. There was no doubt in his mind that Mishti would put in an appearance and he couldn't wait to see the look of astonishment on her face.

Ryan spent the intervening ninety minutes gazing upon the majesty of the mausoleum and complying with a number of peculiar requests from Indian youngsters who, for some reason, wanted to have their photos taken with him. His watch read 11.40 and he waited expectantly near the bench while a jostle of visitors took an unending number of photos. He lowered his sunglasses and studiously scanned a sea of people, hoping that Mishti's pretty face might surface. In his grasp was a small gift-wrapped box containing a necklace he'd bought for her birthday. Brimming with excitement, he rehearsed an apology, detailing the unfortunate reason for being unable to keep in touch.

The sun beat down on the nape of Ryan's neck as he waited. By 12.30 there was still no sign of his Indian sweetheart and, for the first time, his optimism began to waver. Refusing to give up on his dream he hung around for two more hours until the numbing pain of realisation finally took hold. He slipped Mishti's present back into his rucksack and, with a heavy heart, headed for an exit.

*

London Heathrow Airport, 2019

In the ten years after his ill-fated trip to India, Ryan immersed himself in his career as a civil engineer with a large construction firm. He'd long since abandoned his extravagant dream of one day meeting up with Mishti; instead he held their brief encounter as a wonderful teenage memory. In the summer of 2014 he married Hayley, his girlfriend of two years' standing, and was now the proud father of daughter Freya, aged three.

Prior to their scheduled British Airways flight to Istanbul, they had cleared passport control and were nearing the front of a snake-like queue at security. Ahead of them a pretty Asian lady with a pronounced limp snagged her suitcase, prompting Ryan to rush to her aid. The lady turned to thank him but instead a gasp escaped her throat. "Ryan!"

Ryan put a hand to his mouth in astonishment. "Mishti! Omigod … it's really you. I can't believe it!"

Hayley allowed her husband to catch up with someone who was clearly an old friend and continued to follow the line with Freya toddling alongside.

Both Mishti and Ryan were lost for words, oblivious to the chain of people filing past. They each had so much to say but no time to say it. Ryan was first to break the ice. "Um, so what has brought you to England?"

"Oh, I was visiting a friend from university who lives in London now. So, how are you? You have a beautiful wife and daughter, I see."

Ryan was still mesmerised by her loveliness. The intervening years had been kind. "I'm good, can't grumble. Um, are *you* married, Mishti?"

A discernible sadness clouded her eyes. "No. As a matter of fact I never married."

Ryan almost told her that he'd travelled all the way to India to meet her but he didn't want to look ridiculous. Mishti, for similar reasons, didn't wish to embarrass herself by admitting that she had actually believed he would make good on his promises. No longer a boy, he was even more handsome now. Her desolate heart mourned for a life that had never been.

"Oh, did you injure yourself while you were here? I noticed you were limping."

"No, just a car accident ten years ago. I'm fine."

Hayley, who had reached the security scanners, called out to her husband.

Mishti touched Ryan's arm. "Hey, you'd better go. It's been so wonderful to see you again. Such an incredible surprise."

"You too, Mishti." He kissed her gently on the cheek and was in two minds as to whether he should leave.

Though Mishti's heart was breaking, she managed a weak smile. "Go, or your wife might fly without you."

Upon reaching the x-ray machines, Ryan looked over to Mishti for one last time. "Hey, Mishti. Did you ever become a doctor?"

"I did, Ryan. Life is good."

The Pantheon

As was always the case at this time of year, the Pantheon ski lodge was filled to bursting with the great and the good. A convivial party atmosphere was in full swing in the main living area where a youthful Muhammad Ali was teaching Ginger Rogers how to do the Ali shuffle and Dean Martin was manning the cocktail bar. Meanwhile, in a far corner watched by a mustering of British kings, Bob Marley, Oliver Reed and Boris Yeltsin were absorbed in an undisciplined game of dominoes that threatened to drown out William Shakespeare's impromptu recitation of 'Shall I compare thee to a summer's day?'.

Across the hall, the grand library was populated by luminaries famous enough not to need any introduction. Aristotle, Confucius and Nietzsche debated social determinism from a circle of leather armchairs, while Pythagoras bored everyone to tears by droning on about his career-defining theorem.

Yet all was not sweetness and light in the Pantheon: Oscar Wilde, for instance, had gatecrashed a conversation between Ernest Hemingway and Victor Hugo specifically to call the American a raving homophobe. By way of reply, Ernest blew a plume of cigar smoke directly into the Irishman's face.

"Well, you evidently know how to blow a Cuban," countered Wilde with a broad smirk, before turning on his heels and leaving Hemingway almost combustible with anger.

Charles Atlas, dressed in faux leopard-skin trunks, sounded the J Arthur Rank gong, signalling that dinner was due to be served in the dining room. With the air smelling of lit candles and decanted wine, the megastars filed in two by two as if boarding the Ark. They scoured the oversized table for their name cards.

"Ugh! Don't even think to place me next to ghastly Hemingway," Wilde exclaimed, switching his card so he could occupy the chair immediately next to Shakespeare. To his right sat David Bowie, followed by Janis Joplin who had brought a bottle of Southern Comfort to the table. Despite Benazir Bhutto and Abraham Lincoln throwing their hats into the ring (happily only metaphorically in Lincoln's case), it was decided that Dean Martin would orate the pre-dinner speech.

A sumptuous meal catering for the multifarious dietary and religious needs of those seated was served from silver salvers, and the air became thick with the thrum of conversations and clink of cutlery.

Sound asleep in a large wingback armchair, with a note safety-pinned to his pullover, reposed a corpulent gentleman who sported a grey beard. The note stated that he wasn't to be woken and that he would eat later.

No one seemed to recognise the slumbering guest so naturally his identity became a talking point among the diners.

"I believe him to be Socrates," declared Archimedes with firm conviction.

"Certainly not," replied Aristotle. "Socrates' head is every bit as bald as the palm of my hand."

"Karl Marx then," ventured Janis Joplin, joining in the guessing game.

"Not a chance," Aristotle grumbled. "The man has a smile far warmer than anything seen on Marx's miserable face."

"Eureka! I have it!" Archimedes enthused. "He is surely the great Leonardo da Vinci."

"Not so," Victor Hugo observed. "Leonardo's beard is not as dense as this fellow's." Those with an interest took a moment to study the man's beard. It was indeed as thick and as white as a lamb's fleece.

"Then who the Dickens is he?" asked Charles Dickens, keen to drop his own name into every conversation.

"We shall ask him when he wakes," said Shakespeare. "For knowledge is the wing wherewith we fly to Heaven."

"Willy boy, we are already in Heaven," remarked Janis Joplin.

"Forsooth, we art," grinned the Bard, dropping into an Elizabethan way of speaking just for fun.

*

The meal was a resounding success. Appetites were sated and so lost were the diners in their enjoyment that none observed the moment in which the armchair was abandoned by its mystery occupant.

Ginger Rogers was the first to notice the sizeable dent in the recently vacated leather seat cushion. "Hey, everyone! The fat bearded guy has scrammed."

"Alas, without us being able to ascertain his name," Dickens sighed.

"How could he have slipped away unnoticed?" wondered David Bowie.

"Take a look at this!" shouted Muhammad Ali, floating like a butterfly towards the panoramic viewing window. Outside the snow was deep and pillowy, luminescent against the coal-dark sky. A team of reindeers was standing serenely in front of an ornate sleigh and the bearded man, resplendent in his cherry-red outfit and black glossy boots, took the reins.

"Merry Christmas everyone!" he hollered as the luminaries rushed to see him off. And, in no time at all, his sleigh was but a dot among the stars.

"A book doesn't come alive until it is being read."

Kevin Ansbro

Acknowledgments

Rather like an actor receiving an Oscar (and also stealing an idea from Nelson DeMille), I would like to thank the following: my mother and father for getting jiggy with it nine months before I was born; Sir Alexander Fleming for discovering penicillin; Mr Kipling for making exceedingly good cakes; Vincent Van Gogh for reminding me that cutting off one's ear is never a sensible idea; Carly Simon for writing a song about me; *Marvel Comics, MAD Magazine* and the *Encyclopaedia Britannica* for fuelling my childhood imagination; the former Queen of Thailand for smiling warmly at my wife and me from her limousine; Aretha Franklin for teaching even illiterates how to spell the word 'respect'; Raquel Welch for visiting me in a boyhood dream, wearing the cavewoman bikini from *One Million Years BC*; Karen 'Genghis' Holmes and Catherine Cousins for being totally amazing; and finally you, the bookworms who enjoy reading about charlatans and shapeshifters, lovers and leprechauns.

"A writer only begins a book. A reader finishes it"
Samuel Johnson.

Big love to you all!
Kevin

BY THE SAME AUTHOR

Kinnara

(Paperback and eBook)

The Angel in My Well

(eBook)

The Fish that Climbed a Tree

(Paperback and eBook)

An excerpt from

Kinnara

Jao, understanding the need to make the trip more memorable, issued a sporting dare. Sawat loved a challenge and this instantly made him forget his disappointment at not seeing the dolphins. His uncle asked if he was capable of diving down and touching the sea bed: he remembered doing the exact same thing when he was a teenager. Hoping to turn it into an exciting escapade for the boy, he even teased him about the sea spirits who lived beneath the waves. Returning with one stone, a shell or even a clump of seaweed, would offer proof of his success.

Sawat couldn't wait to make his attempt; he was a strong swimmer and could hold his breath for a considerable length of time. Plus, he wanted to impress his uncle who was his only paternal influence since the death of his father.

Jao ensured his nephew donned a wetsuit. Despite the surface temperature being comfortable on such a hot day, the water was a great deal colder the further down you went. Sawat dropped into the sea, clutching a dive torch. He took three shallow breaths then, on the fourth, inhaled as much air as his lungs could manage and disappeared beneath the surface. He found it incredibly easy at first and the seabed soon appeared in the torch's bright beam. Going further, though, was more of a struggle; his ears were collecting unfamiliar sounds and the depths buoyed his body, resisting it with a hostile determination. *Perhaps it's the sea spirits pushing back at me,* he imagined nervously. His fingertips had almost reached the bottom, when, unbelievably, he saw something large move. Sawat redirected the torch: He hadn't imagined it; sitting on the sand was one of the spirits his uncle had warned him about, only this one seemed to be half-human, and half-bird! He had never been so scared in all of his life. Sawat yelped in terror, but only a bubble ballooned from his noiseless mouth. He recoiled and twisted his body so that he could return to the safety of the boat. The water roared against his eardrums. His uncle, meanwhile, was beginning to worry whether he should have issued the challenge in the first place. Sawat seemed to be underwater for a disquieting amount of time. Jao was about to dive into the sea himself, when his nephew burst through the surface with cold fear in his eyes. The boy was shouting and babbling incoherently. Jao dragged him from the water, fearing that some damage may have occurred or that he had been stung by jellyfish.

"Uncle, I saw the sea spirit! I saw the sea spirit!"

Jao was hugely relieved, realising that the kid had simply let his imagination get the better of him. He turned the ignition and allowed the engine to idle. Sawat, though, was still babbling incoherently...

An excerpt from

The Angel in my Well

It was blackboard-dark as I arrived home on Friday evening. Gentle flurries of snow embellished the frigid air and dissolved on my face. I carried a flimsy supermarket bag, filled with cleaning products, which I held between my teeth as I fumbled for the door key. A bottle of Australian Shiraz, tucked under one armpit, threatened to smash to the ground any second.

After spreading my goods like budget raffle prizes across a worktop, I walked into the hallway and clicked the central heating on. Sifting through my burgeoning pile of takeaway menus, the *Royal Bengal* this time, I sat down to make some choices. I really don't know why I do this, because I'm a creature of habit. I invariably select the same dishes, and those dishes already have their numbers heavily ringed in ballpoint pen.

Just as my anticipation of delicious comfort food was causing a Pavlovian reflex, I was aware of a strange caterwauling noise coming from outside the cottage. I padded over to the kitchen window expecting to see a fox, or some similar nocturnal creature, but didn't see anything out of the ordinary.

The sound continued: there most definitely *was* a sound, but despite craning my neck close to the glass, there was nothing in view, just the stand-still silhouette of hostile trees that loomed like spectres. This extraordinary noise seemed to grow louder and sounded like no animal that I could ever imagine. Transfixed, but also fearful, I opened the front door and stepped out into the chilled night air. The sky was crow-black, softened by some lithium clouds that had nestled down for the night. And there it was again, the echo of a nearby voice, almost *human*. But all around me was just the eerie emptiness of my front garden and the wispy blossoms of snow that fell silently from the darkness.

Becoming ever more anxious, I could hear the sound of frantic splashing coming from the direction of the well. Instinct overcame dread and I sprinted across the lawn. I then recoiled in horror at what I saw…

An excerpt from
The Fish That Climbed a Tree

London was under a canopy of darkness by the time the Body Snatcher prepared to leave the warehouse. He punched in the key code, his grisly cargo already bagged up and thrown into the back of his van. Yuri and Pascal trusted him enough to lock up and had earlier taken their leave after paying him the agreed sum of cash.

Under a thin crescent moon that hung like a toenail clipping in the night sky, the man was relieved to rinse his lungs with the damp, brackish air that drifted in from the Thames. He wasn't best pleased that his nostrils, skin and clothes were polluted by the smoky, charcoaled climate of the warehouse; it was an unnecessary add-on to the precise list of things that he had to deal with.

As a phlegmatic man, predisposed to discipline and diligence, he was less than enamoured by the African's incautious method of execution. Setting fire to a victim was as messy as it was inefficient; in his view, a loose cannon such as Pascal was a serious liability in his line of work. Yuri, on the other hand, was more measured and clinical, a person that the Body Snatcher could at least do

business with. In truth he intensely disliked both men but the risk-to-reward ratio was weighted solidly in his favour.

Those two donkeys would've probably dumped the body in the river, he thought as he drove towards Tower Bridge against a glimmer of luxury wharfside apartment blocks lit up like cruise ships above the black mirror of the Thames.

www.kevinansbro.co.uk

Twitter: @kevinansbro

Goodreads: Kevin Ansbro